Book Reviews

Decay of Sorrow by author Jacqueline Garcia narrates the trauma which comes with marrying the wrong person. Esme believes she has found the one for her and is blindly in love with him, so she rushes into marriage, even though he is the ex-husband of her late twin, and it has only been around three months since her untimely demise. She is exhilarated and moves in with her new husband, Bill, but is immediately met with a rude welcome when a woman shows up, claiming that he promised to marry her. Esme is naturally distraught, and Bill does little to remedy the situation. More unsettling circumstances occur, and Esme wonders if she knows who she married. Worsening this situation is the appearance of her sister's ghost, Joanna, who informs her that her sudden death wasn't due to natural causes and that she might also be in danger if she remains with Bill.

The book begins in Esme's therapist's office and employs flashbacks to narrate all she endured while with Bill and how Joanna helped her. The story is dramatic, and there are tense scenes of confrontation as Amanda, the woman Bill promised to marry, does her best to make Esme uncomfortable and get rid of her. Bill also adds to the tension by playing mind games with Esme and Amanda. He is a dodgy character who only cares about his interests and making money in whatever way possible, no matter the consequences. Esme, on the other hand, is naïve and a hopeless romantic who insists on turning a blind eye to Bill's faults until her sister starts communicating with her, which upsets Bill, who prefers she remains oblivious and tied to him.

The story is narrated through an omniscient narrator. Therefore, Bill's evil and conniving thoughts are exposed to readers and the plans Esme makes with her sister behind his back while pretending to still be under his influence are also known. There is also some action, as Esme eventually must struggle for her life. The characters remain consistent throughout the story.

Decay of Sorrow is a novel which blends mystery and paranormal elements to tell the story of a woman's struggle for her peace and sanity when she discovers her husband isn't who he claims to be.

—Gabriella Harrison
Hollywood Book Reviews

In *Decay of Sorrow*, newly wedded Esme Porcher is off with her husband Bill to their new, well, somewhat new, home. Bill lived there before—with Esme's twin sister Joanna, who seemingly died of a natural heart attack. Esme quickly finds out that there is another woman in their new marriage, Bill's assistant, Amanda. Not only does she have this surprise to deal with, but her new husband is acting strangely, and Esme keeps hearing her sister's voice. It turns out the voice is Joanna's invisible ghost. Joanna tries to warn Esme of her fate, but Esme is desperate for her charismatic husband's affections. So much so that she ignores her dead sister's sound advice. Esme makes some foolish decisions, but Bill's other employee, Todd (who happens to be kind and handsome), is there to help her just in time.

Author Jacqueline Garcia writes very descriptive sentences, fully fleshing out exactly how a character thinks or feels. She uses much more adjectives than the typical author. The story, while there is little backstory to the new couple's arrangement, is quite interesting. It starts off with Esme visiting a therapist in the aftermath of her marriage to Bill, so the reader knows right away that she will eventually pull through the ordeal. There is a lot of back and forth with Esme's feelings. She is very unconfident about what choices she should make, but eventually grows in courage. Bill's character is chaotic. One moment he is making his new wife breakfast, and the next moment his temper is flying. He does and says strange things, which not only confuse Esme but the reader as well. The reader eventually finds out that his motives seem to be more psychopathic and crazed than anything else.

It is not clear what time period this story takes place in. Todd addresses Bill, who appears to be his own age, as "Mister Porcher." This is an uncommon way to address someone, especially someone close in age, in modern-day settings. Esme also stays at home and has no career. However, the characters drive cars and use cell phones. So perhaps the word "Mister," as it is written, is just a formality that Bill's authority necessitates, and it is in fact a modern-day story. The title of the book's correlation to the material is also a bit unclear. I speculate that the "decay" portion refers to the several characters that die, while the "sorrow" refers to the ongoing grief and torment that Esme and Joanna both feel. Though Esme and Joanna are twins, they don't have that strong twin connection which is often the case with twins in fact and fiction.

Overall, this is an interesting story with vivid characters. Each person's personality is clear-cut, and the story is unique and written with much description.

—Michaela Gordoni
Pacific Book Review

Mystery and fear; Supernatural activity; Romance; A Villain; Emotional distress; Nightmares. And a damsel in distress. Put these elements all together and you have the essentials of a gothic novel. Author Jacqueline Garcia, with engaging writing, has woven these elements together into a spellbinding tale.

The plot revolves around Esme Porcher, the "damsel" in distress. She, recently, married the widowed husband, Bill the "villain," of her dead twin sister, Joanna. Bill moves her to the house, Meadoways, where he had previously lived with Joanna. Upon arriving, Bill's mood swings from pleasant to disagreeable. Esme, rattled by his behavior, reflects on her situation, "She knew it was too quick for her to marry Bill so soon after Joanna's untimely death." But she loves her new husband and is committed to him.

Add to the mix, a former love of Bill's, the ghost of Joanna warning her sister about Bill, a potential hero who lives nearby, a domestic environment that is oppressive and ruled by an autocratic and malevolent husband and our heroine who is slowly slipping away from reality ... thanks to Bill. Well, you can just imagine the happenings that unfold.

Jacqueline Garcia keeps the story moving along with writing that, in true gothic romance style, is full of suspense, a smattering of creepiness and a little bit of supernatural interference thrown into the mix. Her characters are well-formed, easily identifiable by strong narrative prose which underscores each personality — a despicable husband, suffering new wife, determined ghost, over-the-top crazed lover and an infatuated sweet man waiting in the wings for Esme.

I am a lover of mysteries. I like trying to figure out the villain's end game. I was intrigued by *Decay of Sorrow* because the author does not put that piece of the puzzle into play too soon in the story, keeping readers in suspense as to the point behind Joanna's death and, perhaps, quite possibly Esme's. It would be slightly unfair to both the author and readers to reveal too much of the plot. That would undermine the joy of reading a mystery. What I will say is that Jacqueline Garcia creates enough tension and uncertainty among all of the characters to keep this thriller a riveting read until the story's conclusion.

Reading *Decay of Sorrow* is a little grittier than the average romance novel which makes it a great way to while away an afternoon or as a way to take a small step out of your own day-to-day reality and into a duplicitous ensemble of some truly conniving characters. The storyline is gorgeous, carefully planned, and written in a way that can be deemed perfect.

—Susan Brown
Hollywood Book Reviews

DECAY
OF
SORROW

Jacqueline Garcia

Published in the United States of America

Brilliant Books Literary
137 Forest Park Lane Thomasville
North Carolina 27360 USA

ISBN:
Paperback: 979-8-88945-378-9
Ebook: 979-8-88945-379-6

Dedicated to my family and friends and
Santiago, who is simply the best

Love and tight Hugs

Prologue

"Sometimes it is better to just walk away from things and go back to them later when you are in a better frame of mind."

The therapist's soft gentle voice uttered this course of thought in a calm and soothing tone usually meant for those patients who come to her in an agitated state. Even though she wasn't in such a frantic state of mind, Esme Leona Porcher must admit that she was her therapist's most anxious cases. Why, she had to even bite back this hysterical laughter tickling deep inside her throat, her bright topaz eyes watering and smarting by those very fresh memories that had brought her here in the first place. Had she been truly honest with herself, Esme would have gladly self-confessed that she really didn't want her therapist thumbing through her terribly broken mind and soul through the rotting decay of her guilt and sorrow she still carries deep within her person like a reader browsing through a book. Nevertheless, the other woman's words were, in her opinion, warm and sincere enough for Esme to almost trust her.

Almost…

Esme's stomach churned in protest while her mind, heart, body, and soul noiselessly rebelled against her therapist's most heartfelt advice. Maybe it is the unfortunate aftermath to the poisoning she both unwittingly and unwillingly experienced.

Maybe.

It could be anything, of course, but how can she simply walk away from the awful things that were done to her?

To her older twin sister, Joanna?

To that girl, Amanda?

"You're safe now. He's gone."

Ah, yes, the bogeyman is gone, but not forgotten, a voice contemptuously snarked inside her head even as she made every effort to convince herself of this truth while trying to manage to keep in mind she is really and finally safe from him.

Her husband.

Feeling a fierce headache coming on as a result of merely thinking about him, Esme felt her throat constricted as she measured her words carefully and precisely:

"Is it okay if I go back to my room right now? I don't feel well and I have this pounding headache."

With a worried look splashing across her kind face, the therapist smiled a sympathetic grin and gently closed her notebook, her well-manicured hands clinching to each other in a compassionate and nonthreatening manner.

"Of course, Esme, but always know that I am here for you whenever you need me."

"Thank you."

"I know that you have been through a terrible experience, but I want you to think about what I said, okay?"

"Okay."

As she walked slowly down the hall, carelessly ignoring its well-lit ambiance, Esme allowed her mind to dive deep and wander back to its fathomless well of memories she didn't want to go to, but needed to.

Back to Meadoways, Bill, Amanda, Todd, Joanna, past her twin sister's funeral where she first met Bill and felt both attracted and chosen by him, completely unaware of the dangers that lie ahead for her, leading her here.

One

Meadoways was just as Joanna described it in her letters to Esme. A quaint little cottage-style house, decent in size, two stories, small but not too small. Fit for a small family, it was built on a small hill dotted with oak and magnolia trees where a long winding dirt road strategically slashed through the tree grove like a whip in mid-flick, making a perfect impression to its new mistress. Ashen bluish gray clapboard with a snowy white trim, it is such a modest little two-story creature, sickly and polite. For the woman who became Esme Porcher, she is beyond any doubt and totally swayed that this house is the most beautiful and cute house she has ever seen. Ever since Joanna's funeral, when she and Bill met for the first time, did she sense an indistinguishable yet familiar connection to the shrimpy two-story dwelling in question. Even with its completely glaring five inches-wide cracks clearly showing at the front left side of its basement foundation, it is a strange bond to her late sister nevertheless.

"Well, what do you think?" Bill purred as he turned off the car, his icy blue eyes staring right at her with anticipation.

"It's just like what Joanna described to me in one of her letters. It's so beautiful!" Esme breathed excitedly, her hands reaching out to touch her husband's right arm only to feel slighted when he abruptly yanks his arm away from her at the mere mentioning of Joanna's name. Promptly sensing a sudden chill and restlessness building between them as they remained sitting ever so still in the car, imposing her to blurt out, "Is it ours?"

Automatically she clinched her eyes shut, preparing herself for the angry storm of verbal hits and volleys to be released upon her that seemed to be part of their wedding contract once the "I dos" were said and done. Instead, Bill surprised her with a deep-throated chuckle, pleasing and confusing his wife of just two days right away. Her pretty cheeks reddened in their betrayal of her blushing a hot poker red as his hand crept over to capture and lift her left hand, gently kissing it right where her plain gold wedding band rested comfortably on her third left finger.

There is so much I have to learn about my husband in order for me to be a good wife to him, Esme fancied as Bill softly treated her hand like it was the most precious thing he has ever held in his hot big hand. The same hand he pressed ever so slightly with a hint of possessiveness in his grasp until now, stopping her from grabbing the door handle to open the car door with her free right hand.

"What are you doing, wife?" her husband teasingly growled at her, his eyes full of dancing mischief.

Innocently and totally confused at what he is trying to say, she replied, "Why, opening the car door…why?"

"I thought you wanted to leave me."

Shocked and easily dismayed that she made her husband think that she was leaving him, she cried out, "Oh no! Honestly, I just wanted to open the door. Honest."

"Honey, let me help you out of the car so I can carry you over the threshold, okay, Missus Porcher?"

"Okay, Mister Porcher."

"Good girl.

Possessing a loving smile, Bill Porcher tenderly kissed his wife's warm left check before planting another peck right on her pleased lips, enjoying the sweet sourness of her cherry lip gloss.

"Now, I am going to unlock the door. I'll be right back," he promised.

"Okay," she repeated, this time in a breathless whisper, smiling like an idiot, her brain singing at the top of its ideal imaginary lungs:

Missus Porcher. You're *Missus Porcher!*

DECAY OF SORROW

Snuggling tight against the rich creamy softness of her husband's car's plump yet firm leather car seat, Esme felt sad and guilty all of a sudden at how all of this happened so…rapidly. Yes, that was it: too fast, so speedily she almost felt her head spin out of control. Her sister had only been dead and buried for only two *months* when her devilishly handsome—her sister's words not hers for Esme found Bill to be breathtakingly good-looking—brother-in-law began to astonishingly run after her in a relentless fashion, silently delighting her even as it absolutely destroyed her all at the same time without her realizing it.

Thoroughly enchanted with the fact that she is now Bill Porcher's wife, her very own prized and treasured truthfulness. Gone is Esme Leona Cantrell, quickly replaced by one Esme Leona Porcher as a result of a quickie marriage.

I am now a wife and a Porcher…

"Hello? Hello! What are you doing in Bill's car! Get out of there right now!"

"Oh!" was all Esme could meekly say as she humbly opened the door to get out to stand in front of an angry goddess in human form. At least that is what this woman looked like as she loomed outside the car window. Brilliant and beautiful against the night sky, the woman's stunning beauty was forever twisted in a wild fury while her dark blue eyes snapped and crackled like an enraged almost sapphire wildfire hungrily devouring everything in sight as they glared pointedly at Esme with a certainly noticeable detached interest dancing right along with this intense possessiveness and pride. A little bit older than Esme by a couple of years and more stunning than the younger woman, the older woman convulsively rapped on the half-opened window with her elegant knuckles as if to make a definite point, if not a more obnoxious one. Her exclamation demanding and piercing to Esme's sensitive ears, throwing the younger woman off guard without the usual hemming and hawing.

"How dare you! You're supposed to be dead! And stay dead! You don't belong here…and you don't belong to him! What business do you have here? He's not yours! He's mine! Do you hear me, dead woman? Mine! You...*a dead woman!*"

"Wh—what?"

In Esme's confused point of view, a crazed flurry of information and questions bombarded her stunned mind from every corner imaginable and unimaginable. The most important questions raged and seethed deep within her aching head screeched at high-pitched speed:

Who is this woman? Why didn't Joanna tell me about this woman? Bill belongs to her? How? Why? Do I even know my husband at all? Didn't Bill tell her about me at all?

A feeling of unease, dread, and nausea swept over Esme as this older woman's words decisively struck her, smashing her heart into a million pieces in so many ways possible. This woman, whose hardened eyes and agitated soul squawked of her fierce protection and savage obsession as she continues to scowl minute by ever loving minute while she continued to intensified her uncompromising scowl, leaving Esme to struggle to find her own voice against this angry assault.

"I—well—I—"

"Amanda! What the hell are you doing, bothering *my wife!*"

The woman named Amanda spun around to him, her humanity crumbling through the goddess exterior, her voice shaky and highly pitched, "But she's *dead*! You promise me! You promise to be with me and marry me not *her!*"

Pointing a quivering finger at Esme to prove her argument, whatever that may be in Esme's opinion.

"Amanda..."

"But—"

"Shut up, Amanda, and go home! Now!" Bill roared and just like that, all the bravery and nastiness Amanda ever held for Esme and had maintained for Joanna fell and shattered like glass despite this understandable perplexity for one brief moment on Esme's part. It didn't last long because there is this quirky sense of triumph as Amanda basically curled up her lip like an angry dog, growling out this last sentence much to Esme's horror and dismay:

"Your *wife*! This mousy carbon copy of Joanna? Why did you marry *her* when it's *me* you want to marry? Hmm? You promised to marry me when you buried your first mousy wife! I gave up everything for us to be together!"

Amanda spat out her jealous and hurt venom at Esme, at Bill, at them both, not caring if Bill's mousy wife number two is wounded in the crosshairs of her injured heart and soul. She was about to bury the knife deeper when Bill interfered, his voice harsh and cruel as her own:

"Enough! Amanda, go back to your house *right now*! I will talk to you later, okay?"

"Oh, okay…bye, Little Mouse."

The older woman muttered it under her breath, her jealousy simmered down to a mere fraction of what it was now that Bill ordered her to go home with her tail tucked between her legs. Meanwhile, Esme wasn't feeling so brave or cocky enough to enjoy her husband choosing her. Up till now Amanda's words were clamoring at her left and right with no relief in sight:

Little Mouse…Why did you marry her when it's me you want to marry? You promise to marry me! I gave up everything for us to be together.

The words raced round and round inside her head, once again breaking Esme's heart into a million sharp itty-bitty pieces in the process, shattering her world apart even as…

What?

"Hey, Honey, are you…all right? You look a bit pale."

All right? Do I look all right?

She wanted to scream at her husband until the tears came to wash away the pieces of her heart. Shaken and stirred uncontrollably by this sudden blast of news ripping through her happy moment, all Esme could do was to nod dumbly and not trust her mouth to open for fear of what it might tell him. Her husband, her new husband, had her sister *and* this Amanda woman too? At the same time? Even as Amanda walked away with this huge grin of accomplished triumph at seeing the pained look on Esme's face, the younger woman bent over backwards trying to make any sense in all of this. her heart galloping at full speed, her emotions mauling her insides to bits all the while her mind spat out and threw up her thoughts and questions a mile a minute.

Joanna and Amanda? Did Bill cheat on Joanna with Amanda? Did Joanna know? Will Bill cheat on me too?

Esme wanted so much with all her aching heart and soul to ask Bill only to have a house key casually shoved into her hot little hand, her husband's voice raw and rough with annoyance:

"Take the key and go inside the house. I will explain later, okay?"

Bill Porcher's new bride simply and foolishly nodded, her cheeks warm with embarrassment and heartache, the other woman's bitter words still biting and fresh. Just as much as she naively craved to place confidence in her husband being as pure and innocent like her, Esme finally have to realize there is a meaningful truth which could never be denied or ignored. She is the new wife, striving her damnedest to overcome this acidic blasphemy by knowing better than to doubt her own husband in spite of the fact it would have been easier to suspect him in the first place.

"Esme, get in the house *right now*!"

Scurrying out of her husband's way, Esme sprinted as fast as her feet can carry her, Amanda's falsetto squeals of crude laughter following after her. A damnable blistering howl that is not so easy to ignore nor forget. Racing up the raggedy fissured concrete walkway, up the wide and thick three steps. Up to the strangely comforting presence of the house's nicely polished red oak door whose shiny brass lock effortlessly took in the given key. Turning the matching brass circular doorknob, she hurried inside just in the nick of time to cut off Amanda's overwrought giggling at a desperate speed with a resounding slam of the front door. Generously thinking she can lean on the door for support, Esme was surprised to discover her legs defying, forcing her to slide down into a crouching sitting position with her back against the door in absolute darkness and silence.

Her Bill…

Promising to marry another woman after her sister died *two months ago* and *before her*!

She knew deep within her heart it was too quick for her to marry Bill so soon after Joanna's untimely death, but why? Better yet, her wounded heart insisted, just who is *this* Amanda? Why did he promise her marriage? Does he love her? Are they still seeing each other?

"Why didn't he tell me about this before we got married?" Esme muttered under her breath in the direction of the said murkiness and quietness, completely unaware that she was not totally alone.

"Because he didn't want you to know," a soft feminine voice whispered in Esme's ears, startling her.

"Oh! Hello?"

Esme called out into the darkness only to be net with a hushed stillness all around her, causing her head to spin wildly round and round until she passed out in a dead exhausted faint.

Two

“Esme? Esme! Honey, are you okay?”

Bill’s concerned voice broke through the hazy fuzziness that enveloped Esme in a soft ambiguous blanket as he scooped her up in his arms, cradling her gently while she slowly come back into the land of the wakefulness.

“Oh…my…what happened?”

Her head suffering something really fierce, her eyes being defiant by refusing to open, she struggled to sit up blindly only to meet up with a certain stubborn resistance she couldn’t put a finger on. Oh, the resistance wasn’t threatening; in fact, it felt more like the opposite: warm and comforting. She sensed her voice weakening with exhaustion as she repeated:

“What happened?”

“You fainted.”

“I did?”

Inside her achy and stunned head, Esme struggled to count Bill’s words. Two words. Two measly words that may or may not mean anything in particular. Somehow it did surprise Esme because she had never fainted before in her entire life. With a deep sigh, she gingerly forced her eyes to open, suddenly noticing the worried look dancing across Bill’s handsome face. Particularly all the stress and strain crowding and crumbling around his eyes and mouth.

“Oh.”

Bill smiled a soft genuine grin she could almost but not quite see in the pale darkness, making him look younger than his 35 years. Esme could almost imagine him at an older age when he was in his anxious state. She actually wanted to make this last forever but had some pesky questions that needed to be answered by him.

"Who is Amanda?"

Raking his hand through his warm wheat-colored hair, Bill groaned a shameful grunt, his icy blue eyes emotionless as they kept a frosty glossy stare whilst looking at her with a distinct exasperation.

"Why do you want to know?"

"Because I am your wife."

"That's it?"

"Yes."

Heaving a sigh that was so heavy she swore he was having trouble breathing, her husband simply wrapped his arms around her snugly, his eyes pointedly fixed on the front door in case he needed a quick getaway from the house, Bill started to number crunch the steps from here to the couch to the door. His vocal sound, deep and matter-of-fact, droned on:

"Look, Honey, no matter what Amanda says, *you're* the woman for me. Sure, she works as and she's gorgeous as all hell, but she's not my type."

"Wait a minute…she's your *assistant*? As in she works for you?"

"Yes…so?"

"So? Then why did you promised to marry her?"

Again, that damned sigh came back with a vengeance, followed by the dramatic roll of his icy blue eyes, driving Bill to drawl "Esme".

She drawled back: "Bill."

In a furious admission of his guilt, he stormed, "Oh, all right! I was lonely before I even met you…"

"And you just simply proposed to her *two months* after my sister died?"

"Well, I proposed to you three months after your sister died."

"Bill! That's not the same…"

"Oh, yes, it is. Oh, Honey, please don't worry about Amanda just because she has the hots for me. Believe me, she will cause trouble between you and me so I would stay away from her as much as possible."

"Okay. But what about Joanna?"

"What about your sister?"

"Did Amanda cause trouble between you and my sister while you were married to her?"

"Yes. Look, before you start a fight with me over her, Amanda has a thing for me for a long time. She protects what she considers hers. That's all. So, I wouldn't worry about her."

"Oh…"

"Yeah—oh…"

Regardless of the truth slopping out of the fogginess and into the light, Bill's voice narrated a splinter of stress and agitation combined, something Esme really didn't want him to turn out to be. Even though she braved a tenderized mixture of relief, fear, and happiness at learning Amanda is both a threat and not a threat to her. Amanda's possessive obsession of and controlling attraction to her husband is both real and imaginary all at the same time.

Or maybe it is the selfish romantic in Esme…

Doubt crept in to consume her brain in nerve-wracking thoughts, causing her to pipe up in a kind of childish glee as she wanted to wrap her arms around her husband, hugging him tight, but not dare to:

"So, I am your wife, now and always?"

"Of course. Until the end of time. Now, can I get a hug and a kiss?"

"Sure thing," she purred, happy as a cat with her bowl of cream as she beamed up at him before enthusiastically lobbying herself at him with her heart and arms wide open, kissing him zealously with a hunger she had never knew existed inside her. Cozily and constantly hugging him, exchanging warm wet smouches on his passion-welcoming lips, it helped Esme to gently nudge away all those pesky nagging thoughts about her late sister and the possessive assistant all the way to the back of her mind.

"Honey, I will be right back. Now, come on, don't pout and be that way. I have to handle Amanda with kid gloves in order for her to understand that you and I are meant to be together, not me and her. Okay?"

"Okay."

Esme tried her best to cheerfully agree as she gave him another tight squeeze before reluctantly letting him go. It was all she could do to keep her tears at bay as she realized that Amanda is here to stay as his assistant while she had the upper hand of being his wife.

Yet, it didn't feel right or that way…

"Good girl. Now go upstairs and get some rest or, if you up to it, take a tour of the house. Every room is open and waiting for you to explore them and there are only six rooms to go into."

Prudently concluding that what she is going through is a heated pool of excitement sloshing about inside her quivering stomach, Esme took in a deep breath and enjoyed the thought and hope of actually living in this house where, one day, Bill and she will have a family of their own.

One day…

The snappy click of the front door closing shut brought Esme back to the here and now, leaving her alone with her own company at the moment. Bearing that in mind, she stole this point in time to tour the house just like her husband suggested.

Cautiously and respectfully, she took her time with each room, flicking the lights on and off in due time after each satisfied and utmost care given while soaking each room's individual atmospheres and surroundings. Be that as it may, there was this lack of character that haunted this house completely. A personality of whom her Bill really was inside his home even when he is not around. On second thought, the first five rooms she explored reminded her of a model home instead of a real residence.

"Last but not least…"

Esme wandered over to the second and last bedroom on the second floor where the two bedrooms and a bathroom are located.

Reaching for the doorknob and grasping it firmly, making a slow turn of her wrist, she twisted the knob only to find it locked.

"Locked."

Frowning in total concentration, she tried to turn the knob just to be met with the same resistance once again.

And again.

"I must remember to ask Bill about this locked door when he gets home."

Going back downstairs to the living room, Esme lightly plopped herself down on the plush chili red love seat, a mollifying sigh escaping her lips that seemed to equal with bored and tried patience.

That is, until she saw a vase of flowers standing ever so perfectly right in the middle of the mahogany dining room table.

"Oh, how lovely!"

Strolling over to the table, pleased and confused at the same time, she carefully reached over to the vase and grabbed it, pulling ever so cautiously to her with great care and concern for the flowers and their water. Pushing her nose into the flowers' snowy white bells with a certain wild uninhibitedness that would have made her blush in an undisturbed bashfulness, she inhaled their fragrantly sweet, fresh, almost lemony scent.

"Mmm…even though my favorite flower is the lotus, I can easily make a special consideration for this blunder," she breathed contentedly, leaving the flowers exactly where they are, a sleepy little yawn hurriedly snuck away from her mouth before she could catch it with her free left hand. Slowly she made her way upstairs towards the only bedroom she's allowed to go in. Lying down on top of the bed with a gentle plop, Esme's usually bright topaz-tinted eyes dulled themselves and closed in what she could only hope to be a complete and probably dreamless sleep.

Three

In her defense, Esme really doesn't recall as to how long she slept or even what actually coax her to open her eyes, but she did allow herself to roll out of bed to the delicious smell of rich sizzling bacon and fresh earthy veggie omelet cooking downstairs in the kitchen.

"Mmm," she mumbled happily as she sleepily rose to stand wobbly on her own two feet, steading herself on the edge of the bed, her senses high alert and wide awake to boot. Not quite awake, she missed out on the sight of the closed bedroom door until it was almost too late.

Did I shut the door?

She stopped to stand utterly motionless, wondering against hope that either she or her husband shut the door while her eyes caught the display of the bedroom door being completely closed. Unquestionably, it would make faultless sense since she was apparently totally alone in this house for the whole night.

Or was she?

A sudden invasion of hiccups swiftly conquered her just as Esme let her shaking left hand to touch the bright yellow brass knob in a cagy manner. At this juncture, she is a frightened little bunny when she really wanted to be strong lioness, stubborn and courageous enough to press her own power to scare away any intruder stalking about in their house.

But there is one problem:

Why on earth would a prowler be brave enough to cook breakfast?

It was a silly question had it not been for the actual cooking smells and sounds wafting about inside this house.

That is, until…

"Esme! Honey! I cooked you some breakfast!"

Her stomach rumbled in response and hungry protest, Esme calmly cracked wide open the door, her voice light and cheery as she called out:

"Breakfast? Mmm…good. I'm starving!

Gone went this odd and twisted sense of dread, quickly and abruptly replaced by a hankering so raw and real in both her stomach and head that it coerced her to scurry down the stairs and into the dining room, sneakily stealing a seat at the table so she can stare outside the window opposite from her while relishing her morning meal in peace.

"Breakfast for my love," Bill practically sang out his enthusiasm at having his wife for company and playfully flirted with her as he served her a plate of veggie omelet and two crispy strips of bacon right in front of her, sealing the transaction with a long lingering kiss on the kips.

Famished to a fault, Esme was about to dig into her omelet with a delightful glee when she noticed something missing from the dining room table top.

"Bill, what happened to the vase of flowers that were here on the table? You know, small bells, white flowers, and smells pretty good?"

A frown furrowing his handsome face, Bill appeared to be pondering approximately what the hell she is gabbing about as he gently put his fork and knife down. Staring right at her, his voice low and almost in a confident whisper, he spoke without any warning:

"We have Lilies of the Valley, which is the flower you are talking about and describing. They grow in our backyard, but I haven't cut any of those flowers for the table since your sister died."

His deep voice, usually so strong, broke a small smidgin when he told her of her sister. Of course, she would have argued about the flowers, but shut it down before she made it worse. On the other hand, after taking notice of his low tone whisper, she decided to take the high road. In its place, Esme turned her attentions towards last night and the second bedroom.

"Thank you for shutting my door. Why didn't you go to bed with me?"

"I didn't shut the door. I spent the night on the couch because I didn't want to disturb you," Bill spoke in a matter-of-fact tone, the frown still engraved on his forehead, suddenly reminding her of another thing:

"I took a tour of the house and found one of the bedroom doors is locked. I thought you told me that all the rooms are open for me to explore."

"I *did*? No, you must not hear me right. I use that room for storage and the door must have been stuck…"

"Stuck?"

"Yeah…but don't worry about that room. You don't need to go in there unless you want to."

"No…it's okay…"

Esme glowered at her husband and his choice of words, anxiously keeping in mind how odd and vacant his words really are and were. How weak he sounded in his explanations.

Still, she had to know….

"Okay, Bill, I have a question."

"Shoot."

"What if we decide to have a baby?"

"Are you pregnant?" he demanded; his icy blue glare froze in fury at her as she struggled to make things right with her husband once again.

"No."

His icy blue dirty look melted in a soft wave of blue relief, wounding Esme in such a way that she couldn't even dare to approach it from any angle as he went on, not observing the pained look in her eyes and face:

"Honey, we have only been married for about two weeks—maybe less than that—and you're talking about babies?"

"So, no babies?"

"No—at least not right now," he rapidly spat out with a noticeable shudder that told her one thing: no babies *at all*. In all honesty, she felt her heart shatter into a million pieces once again, forcing her to put on a brave face while trying her best to swallow up that disappointing fragment of news. No kids! Well, Esme took to task at comforting herself with the fact that she could still love him no matter what when Bill's cell phone rang on the dining room table.

Picking up his phone with a sigh, Bill answered:

"Porcher speaking. Todd? Okay. Okay. I will be over there soon. Thank you."

"What's wrong? Who's Todd?" Esme probed, undoubtedly alarmed as Bill tossed his cell on the table top with a skittering thump. Her husband hurriedly drew in his breath before giving the news:

"It's Amanda. She tried to kill herself a couple of hours ago. Todd, her brother, just called me to tell me this."

Startled, she sputtered, "What? How?

Exasperation drove him to grate, "She drank some anti-freeze in her coffee. I told you that she was not right in the head."

His passionate snarl both surprised and disturbed Esme significantly, confusion staying in the deepest corner of her mind and heart all at the same time.

Amanda trying to kill herself over Bill? It doesn't make sense because she seemed so sure and confident of herself that nothing negative could touch her, Esme reasoned as her mind spun round and round in her memory and impression of this Amanda. From what she saw and even noticed of Amanda, there wasn't any sign of the other woman being this love-obsessed woman who was totally engrossed with Bill. Then again, the other woman gave the impression of staying cool, calm, and collected even when Esme first met her, suspected that she was being threatened, despite the obsessive-possessiveness Amanda held for Bill. Nevertheless, it just didn't make any sense because there was so many questions and not enough answers in regards to Amanda. Of course, it was a no-brainer to admit that Bill is handsome and charming enough to make any woman obsess over him, even going so far as to be possessive over him.

But can Bill's handsomeness and charm drive someone in to dying over him?

"Bill, why in the world would Amanda try to kill herself over you?" she asked, bracing herself for an answer that she didn't want to know but had to. It was a question that suddenly made Esme's blood run cold in her veins and arteries as she caught him staring at her in such a dangerously cold-blooded way, she actually thought:

Could Bill drive someone into doing things for him? Sacrificing themselves to Bill in the name of God knows what while no one figures it out? Even me? Is Bill doing these things to me, grooming me into some sacrificial lamb without me realizing it? Or is it too late for me?

His voice emotionless and cruel, Bill snapped, "Esme, how can you be so cruel? So suspicious? A woman nearly dies and you have the *nerve* to ask me and act like it's <u>my</u> fault!

"But…Bill…I didn't mean…"

Her husband's handsome face twisted and turned into this ugly angry dirty look at her, throwing her into some kind of danger without mutable silence out of fear of putting her foot deeper in it.

"Now I am going to the hospital and see how Amanda is doing. Just do me a favor and sit here and eat your breakfast, okay?"

"Oh…okay."

All she could helplessly do is to watch her husband stalk out of the front door, cringing obviously at the angry sound of the door being slammed shut right in front of her. Her stomach twisted topsy-turvy, automatically losing her appetite while something heavy and unforgiving finally settled itself deep inside her heart like a stone dropped in lake water. Each minute, she made sure to keep her eyes fixed on the front door, half-hoping and half-expecting Bill to come home any time soon. Minutes passed, perhaps even an hour or two before she decisively realized he won't be home anytime soon.

Wincing once more, Esme was already cognizant that there might or might not be any talking or cuddling between them *at all*, much less anytime soon. She even waited patiently for the "ha-ha" part, but it never came.

Even now she strived to do her hardest part to believe if he came back and tell her that it was just a poorly thought-of joke, then everything would be all right. But he didn't and that was what shattered her heart into a billion bits and pieces once she concluded it is all too real and true. Maybe if Esme had fallen into stupidity or shock, things would have been different between them right now at this very moment. On the other hand, she really wasn't so sure for the reason that she had never been in shock before.

Esme felt burning hot scalding tears swimming and stinging in her eyes while repeating these words neurotically and firmly:

'I'm sorry…I'm so sorry…"

The waterworks fell without restraint at the same time as she plopped herself on the love seat, plunking her forehead down upon its velvety soft plush cushion. Sobbing her tender heart out as she collapsed deeply into the love seat's supple plushiness.

"I'm so sorry."

Her heavy river of tears thoroughly stained the pleasantly squishy and plump velveteen cushion a good-sized wet spot that eerily jogged her memory of a fresh blood stain and strangely of her husband's involvement in Amanda's near loss of life despite not possessing any provided proof. Horrified by the look of this cruel reminder, she scurried back to the bedroom she slept in like a terrified little mouse running from a cat.

Plunging her entire body on this unfamiliar bed, Esme blubbered her eyes out to the refrain of *Lord what a sad joke this has become* spinning round and round inside her head until she plummeted into a bottomless sleep. As she dropped off into slumberland, she was aware of not dreaming at all with the minor exception of her raven hair being gently stroked over and over in a comforting manner. Kind of like a mother tenderly consoling her child, it is a sweet-tempered caress, one that made her fall deeper and deeper in a peaceful sleep.

A nice, restful, harmonious snooze…

"Esme! Oh, God, Esme!"

Coming across a sudden plunge from the heavens only to end up being slammed down into the land of reality, groggily as she can be.

"Bill? Wha—what are you doing here? Why aren't you at the hospital with Amanda?"

"Honey, it's six o'clock at *night*. Amanda's been stabilized and should be home tomorrow. When I got home and found you lying ever so still in bed, I thought something bad had happened to you. I even checked your pulse and you were still out like a light. You've been sleeping for *hours*!"

"*Hours*! How?"

"I don't know, Honey. What made you sleep so long?"

"Well, I have been crying a lot so I cried myself to sleep."

"You cried yourself to sleep?"

"Yes."

"Oh."

Bill's handsome brow furrowed into a concentrated frown as he tried his damnedest to understand his new wife's odd answers. To him, crying oneself to sleep brought about a kind of weakness that despaired him more than ever before.

"Oh, Esme…"

Clenching to him strongly as if for dear life, Esme wailed, begging with all her heart and soul, "Can you please stay here with me, Bill? *Please.* Can you please sleep in the same bed with me? *Please.*"

"I—can't," he stammered, clearly embarrassed by Esme's whiny pleading as he yanked himself free from hot sweaty grasp.

"Why not? We're married," she hissed, her face crestfallen and hurt.

"Esme, please stop pushing me!"

Bill angrily pushed her away as he stormed out of the front door, his anger helped him to slam the door shut once again while she looked forsaking on, her heart screaming out at him what her mouth could not do:

Then why did you even marry me?

Four

The next morning conveyed the impression to Esme that she must walk on eggshells, a feeling she really didn't want to go through at all. Bill slept in the living room once again and made sure to leave her all alone to her own devices in the bedroom. Only this time there wasn't any delicious smells of Bill's cooking because he has most likely gone to work or to the hospital.

A soft creak captured Esme's wayward attention, coaxing her to yell "hello" out loud despite knowing without checking that she is definitely all by herself. Being reasonable, she should have admitted to herself she is all alone and no one would have the guts to come in and rummage through the house with her in it.

At least she hoped so…

"Hel—hello?"

Esme winced at how silly she sounded as she once again called out to whomever and no one at all. She took her time waiting. One minute, then two, then more minutes came and went into hours right along with the pleasant ticking of the living room grandfather clock. Another squishy squeak followed, answering her quietly, causing her to suck in her breath so hard out of absolute fear that her lungs hurt.

Silence rushed in once more. Not some cozy quietude but one eerie in nature. Regular like clockwork, Esme bided her time before giving off one more squawk.

"Hello? Please answer me!" she yowled in total terror like some angry cat, not giving a single damn if she was whining like a startled child.

Truth be told, she only wanted to feel safe and secure in this house, that's all. Nevertheless, it was this stillness that responded to her once again, its bullheaded brazenness definitely not giving a damn to her needs and demands right now, just happily sowing the seeds of fright deep within the confines of her pulverized heart.

"Esme…"

Her name murmured in a hushed breathy tone, startling her, bringing her to shriek loudly not hopeful of anything to *not* materialize in front of her or to her while her nerves remained on edge:

"Hello?"

Nothing.

Then…

"Hel—hello?"

She would have dared herself to open the bedroom door and step out of her new room had it not been for something with heavy feet sprinting over to the door. Squeaking in horror, Esme twisted the lock to locked as she scooted over to cower at the farthest corner while the door started to shake and rattle, knocking wild frantic thwacks on the door's wooden body and desperate turns of the doorknob.

"Stop it…stop it…*stop it!*"

Hands tightly clamped over her ears, Esme wailed these two words till she's gasping and hoarse, her entire body and mind growing ever so lethargic from the energy drain, scaring her even more so. Exhausted by the torment, darkness swept up instantly, swallowing her up whole even as she fainted dead away on the floor, her head smacking hard against the rough white oak slat flooring.

Esme didn't know just how long she had been out cold when she woke up. Her head throbbing something fierce, her eyes dry and itchy, she found herself lying on the bed, a sheet sensibly covering her all the way up to her chin.

"*Ow.*"

"Welcome back to the land of the living, Missus Porcher—Ma'am," grumbled a deep yet soothing masculine voice, his slightly detached tone stirring her up a little more than she is prepared for. Taking a crack at moving up and out of her bed, Esme pushed against the large strong hands that firmly placed themselves on her shoulders. Forcing her slightly down on the pillows and mattress as if she was a sick child who is anxious to go out and play.

"Oh no, you don't, Ma'am. It looks like you might have a nice goose egg on your head. You might feel like you had your head knocked around all over the place. So you need to rest."

"Yes, Doctor. Say, who are you?"

"Close your eyes."

The brilliant light struck her closed eyelids, forcing her to moan and squawk in return. When she finally opens her eyes, she gasped out in surprise and appreciation. Standing by her bed was the most handsome-looking God she has ever seen. Tall, muscular but not too muscular with a golden tan that didn't seem to be sun-kissed, hazel eyes, and bluish black waves of hair, the man was breathtaking, almost too breathtaking for someone as mousy as her.

"Hello," she yelped to which the god smiled shyly and replied:

"Hello. You should be okay."

He shrugged his shoulders as if it was no big thing. In his honest opinion, it really wasn't any big deal at all, forcing the pretty little bird to declare:

"Thank you, Mister—"

"You can just call me Todd."

"Todd? As if Amanda's brother, Todd?"

Shock hurriedly overpowers her as Esme decided to keep quiet in order to keep this blistering headache under some kind of control while he stood there, staring at her with unwavering hazel eyes. At least she wasn't arguing with him nor was he looking as if to start a fight with her. And while the pain is simmering, she tried her best to notice him at a closer peek, much to her somewhat guilty pleasure. Nevertheless, had her headache gone away and her mood was just a little bit better, she would effortlessly wiggle it off as nothing at all and seek a friendship with this god.

That is, if she was smart enough…

"Todd's a good man. You should trust him, Esme."

Again, that whispering feminine voice tickling in her ear, causing her to ask him:

"Did you say something?"

"No."

"Well, I thought…oh, never mind. So, are you going to tell me just exactly what happened to me when you found me?"

"No."

To her ears, Esme thought that she heard Todd's voice hardened so disagreeable and abrupt in timbre that she felt like some chastened child and common outsider than the respected lady of the house."

"No more questions, Ma'am?"

Ah, she heard the strained humor in his voice. She was undeniably certain about it.

"Please call me Esme. No."

"Have you heard of a woman named Joanna?"

"Yes, she was my twin sister."

"What is it? What's wrong?"

"I think this house may be haunted."

There. She said what might have sounded plausible in her head short of providing any proof, something she would not dare to admit it to herself and yet it was there: the creaks and the whispers. Something she doesn't dare to take it back without sounding anymore crazier than she already declares. Nor did it matter Todd was now watching her with a cold skeptical stare as he roughly pulled himself back from her not out of fear but reluctance.

"Haunted? This house? Like ghosts roaming all around and stuff like that?"

"That's the only 'haunted' I can think of and know of."

"How hard did you hit your head?" Todd grilled, tamping down any and all responses, one of those responses being able to burst out laughing, that might either help or hinder this newfound relationship out of fear of hurting her and ruffling her feathers with him and his scoffing ways.

"Damn it, Todd! It's not funny! This house is *certainly* haunted!"

"Do you have any proof that this house is haunted?"

"No, but…"

"Then I think that it is better to not mention this to Mister Porcher. He will not be as…understanding as I am."

"Understanding about what? What's going on, Todd? Esme?"

"Nothing, Bill."

"Nothing, Mister Porcher."

For once in her married life, Esme defied her husband by keeping her pretty mouth shut.

"Come on, Esme, what the hell is going on?"

"Well—"

"Ma'am—"

"I think this house is haunted," she blurted out, much to Todd's chagrin as Bill's knee-jerk reaction to this awkward exchange was to explode into a flat hollowed out laughter, forcing Esme to become furious with her husband and his jeering ways.

"Bill!"

"Mister Porcher—"

"What? I don't believe in this supernatural crap and I am not sorry for admitting it, okay? Just drop it."

"But there is a ghost in here—"

"Esme, drop it *now.*"

"—and Todd may not believe me, but I thought *you would*!"

"Todd?"

"Yes, Mister Porcher?"

"Amanda will be home from the hospital tomorrow. If you value your home and Amanda's job, you will leave this house and not bother my wife ever again, okay? Forget everything you have seen and heard right now."

"Bill…"

"*Right* now."

"Yes, sir. Ma'am."

Esme's heart plummeted and freefall right into her stomach as she watched Todd leave her bedroom door. Tears burned scorching hot in her eyes as she hopelessly watched him disappear into the darkness, forever lost to her.

"Bill…"

"You are not to associate with Amanda and Todd, okay?"

"Why?"

"Because I said so."

"But the ghost! It rattled the door and doorknob! I swear!"

"Honey, just drop it…okay?"

"No!"

"Esme…"

A wild stream of tears flowed down her cheeks as the man she loves mocked and even threatened her just because he didn't possess any confidence in her and her ghostly encounters. Seeing her tears, Bill loudly sighed and silently admitted a sudden if not temporary defeat now burning right in the very core of his own cynical soul.

"Did you really see this ghost?"

"Kind of…no."

"Which one is it: kind of or no?"

"No."

"No!"

"Then explain the door and knob rattling, huh?"

"Simple. It was a breeze. This house is eighty years old."

"A breeze?"

"Yep, a breeze."

"Get out" was all Esme could say and stand at the moment while a hasty flash of her husband's smug mug infuriated her even more so. She flung open the bedroom door even wider until it could almost hit the wall, her voice full of hurt and anger as she screamed:

"Get out, Bill! Go sleep on the couch since you are so very comfortable sleeping there anyways! I'm going to bed. Good night!"

"Esme…Honey…"

"Good night!" she growled one last time as she slammed the door shut before he could try to sweet talk his way back into her good graces. Right now, as far as she is concerned, it will be a cold day in Hell before if and when she would ever forgive him.

Five

I f this day promised to turn out better than yesterday, Esme hopefully presumed to enjoy the quiet solitude of cleaning the house—her house—from top to bottom without any ghostly incidences or encounters. A good thing since Bill already went to work before she got up. Seizing things as they were last night, she must confess at being happy to *not* see her husband at all due to her being hurt by his cynical butt. Perhaps if she has cooled down earlier, she justly would have forgiven him despite wanting to be childish for only a little while longer.

Just a little bit…

"Bill's not to be trusted."

Oh. no…

Stopping mid-step on the stairs, Esme's heart leapt with both joy and dread all at the same time once she listened to the soft voice on the stairway. Shaking her head in refusal, she maintained to take one step down at a time till she reached the last stair and turned around to face the dining room.

And gasped.

Standing right in the middle of the dining room table was a clear vase filled with water and Lilies of the Valley, startling Esme to the point of tripping down the last step and falling to the floor.

They're back!

Happiness and uneasiness ebbed and flowed deep inside her heart. For some odd reason, Esme had to fess up she really did miss those flowers as if they were old friends.

"So, I am not as crazy as Bill thinks I am!" she crowed to herself, hugging herself in the process.

"No, you were never crazy," the soft voice verified without any argument.

"Hello?"

As soon as she yelped out that word, Esme hurriedly slapped her small hand over her astonished mouth out of distress of being discovered muttering this word of greeting by Bill. Then again, she knew somewhere in the back of her mind her husband was away at work. A reasonable concept, of course, but she still managed to feel so very uncomfortable at such a thought.

An undemanding moderate click emerged from the locked bedroom door, its delicate sound loud enough to scare the living crap out of her in return. Urging her to climb up the stairs ever so carefully and slowly, halting every two steps along the way.

Pausing along the way to the now unlocked bedroom door, Esme chose to be brave enough to let her hand creep up to the doorknob, finally gaining an adequate amount of courageousness and risk to test the door, her curiosity awoken and active. For as much as Esme wished and wanted the door to be locked, she was amazed to find the doorknob not giving her any resistance, letting her turn the smooth knob and push the door without any strange incidents.

"Welcome to my room," the voice piped up just a little bit louder as if proud of this area.

"Your room?"

By any means the room itself looked perfectly and unusually clean. Almost too spotless. No signs of cobwebs, dust, or life dwelled anywhere inside the room. It was just an empty room with a trunk settled over in the far-left corner. Pale blue like a robin's egg, it was nicely complimented by a creamy white trim and closet door, the room was considerably smaller than Esme could ever imagined while she grabs hold of the time to admire the flattering manner of the colors pay tribute to each other, the walls matching well with the trim without any truly dramatic fuss. Slight in its spaciousness, she must admit that it is odd for a storage room not to contain any storage. Even the closet is vacant.

Except for that trunk…

It seemed only palpable as Esme took her time strolling around this unfurnished bedroom soundlessly listening to the ever-soft creaks and petulant moans her footfalls made while feeling the vast bareness of this tiny room. Stillness swirled all around her even as she continued to try to find answers from this room fruitlessly.

"Hmm…"

Nothing.

Nothing at all…

She was about to leave the bedroom when something heavy dropped with a thick thud close to her left foot. Surprised, she figured that the trunk id only a few feet or so away from her, thinking that it was just her imagination. Looking down, Esme was also clearly flabbergasted to find a 2-inch-thick book nestled ever so close to her foot. Confused and bewildered, she picked up the book and became conscious upon her cautious examination that it is a plain red wine-colored journal. With great care, she sensibly opened up the book to its very first page and found the owner's name handwritten in a familiar flourishing cursive:

Joanna Teresa Porcher

"Joanna…Teresa…Porcher. My twin…"

Over and over Esme mumbled these five words as if reciting a prayer out of shock, her heart pounding and her mind racing a million miles a minute. Snatching the journal closed and tucking it under her arm, for protection, she rushed out of the bedroom without so much as a backwards glance. Turning around, she was going back to shut the bedroom door as if in afterthought when she noticed the door lightly and nonchalantly draw itself closed as if by a supernatural hand.

"Thank you…*Joanna*?"

A soft tap-tap on the closed door let Esme know that she is warmly welcomed by her older twin sister's ghost. Not knowing if she was scared, grateful, or both, all that should matter to her is if this really occurred, this ghostly chance meeting, now she was almost sure as to what to do.

DECAY OF SORROW

I won't tell Bill. I will just act normal so he won't know about Joanna, she vowed to herself in silence even as her excited mind squealed at a happy shrill, bringing on this tremendous headache, forcing her to run into the bathroom to throw up in the toilet with as much force as her stomach could impose. Her stomach hurting in cramps and strains, it wasn't as terrible as this idea of lying to Bill, but it still hit her and her stomach like a ton of bricks, making her struggle to deal with this sneaky little fact.

Hurling up once again, Esme rested her warm forehead against the chilly surface of the toilet's glaring white body, intense searing passionate tears spilling down her sickly pale cheeks even as she strained to stay logical with every neuron of her brain until she honestly thought smoke was going to come out of her ears.

Esme deemed herself as better, but she also felt worse all at the same time. At least, she rationalized, she had about four more days till she needed to go back out there and find work even though Bill argued that he makes plenty of money for them both.

At least…

"I better lie down," she grumbled to herself as she dragged her very exhausted butt over to her bed, plunking herself onto her still somewhat queasy stomach right on the silky soft covers without bothering to pull these covers back. On a spur of the moment, an unaccountable fever promptly engulfing Esme, depriving her of any kind of warning, rendering her to feel as if she's on fire. The journal, secured firmly in her hot clammy hands, unexpectedly fell away from her hands and skidded itself under the bed. Whether or not that is a good thing is clearly unknown, with the major significance that this was done by a supernatural hand.

In her feverish state, she swore she dreamt of her older sister, sitting by her side on the bed, full of life and love as she gently stroked Esme's hair, her voice confident and full of hope:

"Shh… it's all right, Esme."

"Promise?" Esme croaked, her throat dry and aching, the pressure of her older sister's hand clenching hers more pronounced and heavier in her answer.

"Promise."

Joanna's peaceful feminine voice blew that word across her younger sister's scorching forehead in a pleasant yet cooling caress just like a mother would do in comforting and caring for her sick child. Keeping her eyes tightly shut, Esme allowed her twin sister's now freezing hand to lightly stroke her forehead and hair without any whimper or protest from Esme as the younger twin rolled herself onto her back. In response Joanna's hand kept right on stroking her younger twin's forehead and hair until she was absolutely certain that Esme had finally fell fast asleep, Esme's fever flushed scorching and swift like a wild fire.

"Save me, Joanna. Please…"

"I will always be here for you, Esme. I have to save you from him."

"From who?"

"Why, from Bill, of course. He is the one who killed me."

"What?"

Esme came around with that word sounding off as a small scream huddling in midair while she sat up out of the blue like a shot, her sister's claim rattling all over the place deep inside her head, and her bedroom bathed in complete pitch darkness. A weighty kind of anxiousness distressed her during all the time she sat in the murkiness all by herself, restless and feral in her own rampart thoughts. Up to now she only focused on herself when she should have concentrated on him.

"Bill…"

Her fever broken, yet it was her fever being the one to set up this supernatural contact with her older sister, now firing up her mind for the second thing, that of her husband. Up till now the second thing was not whole because it involves the plan of Joanna saving her from Bill.

But that's impossible, isn't it?

Isn't it?

So, what really happened to Joanna and how is Bill wrapped in this with her?

DECAY OF SORROW

It was the only question Esme really didn't have any answers to or information about, leaving her stuck in the murky waters and deep shadows of being misunderstood and misinformed.

"Honey, are you awake?"

Bill rapped softly on the bedroom door, giving Esme enough leeway to address him properly. Keeping a brave face, she mustered up plenty of courage to compel herself to keep her voice even, loving, and steady as usual:

"Yes."

"Can I come in and turn on the light?"

"Sure."

"Close your eyes."

"Okay."

Forcing her eyes to screw up real tight, they still didn't shut out all the intense creamy buttery yellow brilliance of the bedroom light glared through her snugly shut eyelids here and there, coaxing a little squeak of annoyance, much to the swift delight of her husband.

"Bill!"

"I told you to close your eyes."

"I did!"

"Poor baby. Shall I kiss your closed eyes?"

'Yes, please."

Her stomach twisted and turned itself into curls and knots just as Bill tenderly kissed each relaxed eyelid with as much love as he could possibly give. Esme shivered in both terror and anticipation as she allowed him to kiss her keenly on the lips.

"Esme would it be too much if I sleep here? Please?"

"Oh, Bill," she drawled, blushing furiously and giggling quite recklessly.

"What? Why are you laughing at me? "he fiercely demanded, his feelings hurt and stinging.

"Bill! Come back here please!" Esme objected as she watched hopelessly and helplessly Bill sweeping himself off the bed, seething and growling at her before stomping out of the bedroom with an enraged slam of the door behind him.

"Oh, Bill," she wailed into the heavy darkness that sneakily swallowed the house's sleepy insides whole. As she free fall into this darkness, Esme could've sworn that she heard her sister's moan lurking about.

Six

"You shouldn't invite him into your bed."

Joanna's anguished voice broke into Esme's drowsy aching head. It sounded sharp and stressed with a mixture of fury and misfortune.

"I had no choice in the matter. He would have figured it out. Besides, he didn't sleep in my bed last night because I insulted him by laughing at him., "Esme mumbled weakly, flinging her right arm over her eyes to avoid the frosty glare coming from her ghostly twin. "After all, what am I supposed to do if you were in my place?'

"Probably do the same thing as you," Joanna agreed with a resigned sigh, unreservedly putty in Esme's hands with an understanding she would have spent those very same moments just as her younger twin sister has done. On the other hand, Esme still didn't get the point by any means necessary. In fact, she simply felt stuck in the middle of two warring fractions who apparently didn't care about her needs and wants just as long as one of them wins.

"What do you really want from me, Joanna? Why are you here? You're a dead, a ghost, so why me? Why now?"

Esme's voice, cracked and fraught with feral emotions as she plunged headlong into this strange vat of potential mystery, murder, and whatever else is going on in this damned house. She so much wanted

to trust her husband with all her heart and soul, but the ghost of her sister is making things worse between Bill and her.

"To save you from Bill, Esme. Look, just read my journal and don't let Bill know you have it, okay?"

Joanna's journal…

"Shit!"

With an abrupt overstrung cry, Esme hurriedly hopped out of the bed, clad in an overlarge tee shirt and underwear, a frantic determination so to speak, and started to search the bedroom from top to bottom for her sister's missing journal only to find nothing. Since Bill is most likely at work according to the alarm clock by her bed, she figured she can thoroughly go through every inch and foot of her bedroom.

"No journal…"

"Look again."

Esme combed over the bedroom once again and…

"Found it!"

Thankfully discovered, the journal appeared heavier by weight in her shaky hands. Esme soundlessly considered all her options right along with Joanna's journal, too afraid to open it up and read its contents right at this very moment.

" I—I—can't. sorry."

"You have to!" Joanna shrieked, pleading with all her ghostly might. *"Esme…you don't want to end up like me, do you?"*

Esme shook her head, but still refused to open the journal, forcing Joanna's hand.

"Okay. Since you don't want to read my journal, I will tell you: the doctor said that I died of a heart attack…."

"But you were always healthy as a horse!"

"I know! Right? I was healthy one minute then I drink some nasty tasting tea only to drop dead from a heart attack!"

"Well, it can't be genetics, right?"

"You really need to read my journal."

"Why do you believe it is Bill? Do you really think it was him?"

"Oh, I don't think *it's Bill. I* know *it's him!"*

Esme had to choke back those pesky carried away giggles of disbelief as she attempted to do her best to grasp her older sister's words into serious consideration.

"How?"

"The last incident I brought to mind was Bill fixing me break-fast and serving hot tea. He was absolutely insisted that I drink all of my tea. Saying that it will make me feel better because I felt really sick the night before. The tea I drank was bitter and…earthy? Yes, bitter and earthy. You better go and get dressed. Don't want Bill to come in and become a horny dog."

Esme chuckled, replying in kind, "Bill's at work. We have the house all to ourselves."

"Bill works now? Hmm…interesting."

"Why is that interesting?'

"Because when I married him, Bill inherited his father's money and didn't have to work."

"Really?"

"That's right. Now, get dressed and read my journal. Just don't let him see it, okay? If he sees it, you might be in danger. Look at Amanda."

"What about Amanda? She didn't die! Not even a heart attack! According to Bill, she made a suicide attempt."

Exactly! 'According to Bill'. Amanda is a strong-willed albeit spoiled woman who gets in your face before you could even get out of the car."

"How did you know?"

"I watched."

"You…watched?"

"Yes."

"But—"

"Let's get back to Amanda, okay? What I am trying to say is that Amanda is too confrontational and too proud to make a suicide attempt after getting in a scuffle with you. Mind you, not all strong-willed women are spoiled and proud. But maybe she had suicidal ten-dencies without our knowledge, but it just seemed strange, doesn't it?"

"Yes, it does. So what is written in your journal?"

"Mundane stuff. Stuff where things started to get really strange between Bill and me. Look in my journal."

"That really helps, Joanna."

"Just read my journal…please?

"Okay."

Casually cracking open the journal right in the middle and saw…nothing. Disappointed, she grumbled as she tossed the blank journal on the bed:

"There's nothing here. No writing."

"What?"

"Look," Esme retorted, flipping the vacant pages in front of her and her sister.

"Why that sneaky—of course she would do this—"

"Who?"

"Who else? Amanda."

"What are you talking about?"

"Esme, look at it this way: Amanda knew about my death and figured that I should have a diary or a journal. She needed leverage."

"Leverage for what?"

"Why, to marry Bill!"

"What?" Esme screeched, not having confidence in her ears.

"Listen to me, Esme. Please. Amanda put two and two together and brought up the correct number. She snooped around in my room without Bill noticing, stole my journal, stole my journal, read it, took whatever clues out of it, bought another journal that looked just like it, blackmailed him for marriage, and when he agreed, gave him a blank journal in return."

"But Bill didn't marry her; he married me!"

"Precisely!"

"So, Amanda freaked out, Bill poisoned her and made it look like a suicide attempt? I don't believe but I do believe it. It's too clean cut and easy to solve."

"But, Esme, he killed me and she figured it out! He didn't get caught! So how the hell did anything get solved?"

"That's one way of thinking, Joanna, because Amanda is or was blackmailing Bill doesn't mean he tried to kill her."

"True, but what is the other way?"

"I don't know. Amanda may have done it?"

"And try to do herself in? I don't believe it."

"Me too…"

"Well, whatever it is, you still need to watch out or you will end up like Amanda or me."

"Hmm…"

Even though Esme couldn't read Joanna's journal from front to back, she strained herself to glimpse for any clues on what appears to be a blank slate. Clues that might scream out "Bill killed Joanna" or "Bill tried to kill Amanda" only to be strangely disappointed and disillusioned with the fact that there were no such clues after all. At first, Esme was so very enthusiastic at being converted into a sort of detective in her own mystery story, danger be damned.

"What?"

"Nothing…just nothing."

"Maybe. Maybe not. It's possible that Bill cleaned up his tracks regarding Amanda and me."

"It looks like it, Joanna. Then again, why did he lock up an empty room if he had already cleaned up his tracks?"

"But, Esme, he really didn't lock up an empty room. There is an empty trunk in the farthest left corner, remember?"

"Oh yeah!"

"I just don't want you to look at the journal and ignore every-thing else."

With a renewed fire burning hot and proud in her heart and belly, Esme raced over to the empty room's closed door and turned the knob ever so prudently.

Locked!

"Damned it!" she raged, kicking the locked door with her left bare foot, hurting her big toe in the process. Out of frustration and irritation, she limped over to her bedroom, snatched the blank journal off the bed and tossed it in the trash can in the bathroom, where she thought it belonged. However, Joanna didn't agree and somehow managed to save it from its fatal fate.

"Why are you keeping it?" Esme wailed, her toe throbbing a mile a minute as she limped over to sit on her bed. "The journal is empty! There's nothing we can do with it! Besides, it doesn't prove Bill's guilt."

"Ah, but it does, Esme, don't you see? This could be our bargaining chip just it was Amanda's. Amanda was almost killed for this journal and she used it to extort him. Heck, I doubt if Amanda has actually read it at all."

So, it is probable that Amanda lied to Bill about reading it and merely told him that there's incriminating evidence written in your journaling order for him to tie the knot with her?"

"Yes. Then he met you and got hitched to you out of either love or hopelessness or both," Joanna answered, her voice hardened with the truth, causing Esme to recoil in pain and horror.

"Ouch. That was very harsh and very stupid of her. But there's another hitch."

"What kind of hitch?"

"Bill didn't harm Amanda because he was home with me."

"Are you sure?"

"Yes…no…wait. Bill *said* that he needed to talk to her. When I got up, he said that he slept on the couch so he wouldn't wake me up."

"Hmm…so he says."

"Plus, the Lilies of the Valley and their vase are missing from the dining room table when I got up. He told me that they were a figment of my imagination. Basically."

"No, they're not."

"Why did you say that?"

"Because I was the one who put those flowers on the table."

"Did you see Bill come home? Toss the flowers in the trash?"

"No, I was resting."

"Wait…ghosts rests?"

"Yes, we rest. What do you think? That we haunt our specific places 24/7? We need energy to survive and live on and work on just like mortal human beings."

"So, we both don't know if he, Bill, did it?"

"I wouldn't put all my eggs in one basket. In all honesty, I still wouldn't trust Bill with you."

"So, I am still in danger?"

"I'm afraid so."

"Great."

"Sorry."

"Don't be, Joanna. I just have to make sure that I don't even mention this journal to him and hide it from him."

"I think that is a good idea."

"What's a good idea?"

"Bill! You scared me! Don't do that!"

Esme scrambled to hide the journal under her butt while acting surprise when she actually felt scared. Bill hanging outside her bedroom door, forcing her to play stupid, acting like she didn't hear him.

"What, Esme?"

"What?"

"What's a good idea?"

Oh—changing the wallpaper here in the bedroom."

In her estimation, the wallpaper is okay. A simple patterned design of old sailing vessels and old-fashioned anchors dotting a creamy background. Nevertheless, it was in her impulsive opinion that it really should go.

"What's wrong with it?" Bill inquired; his icy blue stare forever trained in on her wide topaz gaze before leaning down to kiss her passionately on the lips.

"It's fine for a little boy's room or a family den, just not for a master bedroom. I was thinking a splash of cream paint will make this room beautiful."

She felt herself slink into the heavy shadows of her mind as her eyes caught the sight of Bill's handsome face souring at the mere mentioning of a family, her heart sinking more than she expected. everything had to be done in a moment's time to save herself from whatever curse has struck her in the first place regarding lying to her husband. Nevertheless, she hoped against hope he will quickly agree so she can get him out of the room as she possibly can in order for her to hide the journal successfully.

"Well, Bill? What do you think?"

"I think that it will be fine as long as I pick the paint color for the room, okay?"

"Deal. Now why are you home so early?"

"Honey, it is almost six o'clock in the evening right now!"

Oops…

"Silly me…so it is."

Esme 's mind scurried in horror and desperation as she struggled to discover how to get her lies in order, only to fail miserably even as she scooted the journal under a blanket while in the act of sitting on it. She relaxed if only for a tiny bit, completely unaware that she was growing pale and sickly yet again.

"Are you okay?"

"Yes…of course…why?"

"You just seemed…off."

"Oh, I think I have been sleeping too long. That's why I am off."

"Hungry?"

Her stomach growled in answer to his question, making Bill laugh good-naturedly in return. Smiling up at him, she experienced a warm flame burning in her heart.

"Of course."

"Come on."

I really must remember to keep track of the time, Esme noted as she followed him out of the bedroom, other questions chasing after her:

Did he hear us talking? Or did he hear me talking?

Seven

What do you mean that he might be involved in this? One woman has died, another woman is in the hospital, and you think Bill might be implicated? How dare you!

Esme could almost hear the annoying clicking of her mind's sharp imaginary tongue on what seemed to be its subjected displeasure, its tempo beat giving away an undisturbed incredulity she knew all too well. She also realized she must ignore her mind's acidic tongue clacking as politely as it ought to be…just not openly.

So, she did the way she could:

She did it covertly.

"Shh…it's okay, Esme. You have the blank journal and will find a safe place for it somewhere," her pep talks to herself continued.

Damn it! The journal!

Jumping up as if her butt was on fire, Esme swiftly snatched up the body-warmed journal located under her left hip and shoved it between the mattresses. Discouragement seeped throughout her heart as she sensed this feeling of total loss and abandonment. Trapped in a house with a potential murderer, she was fast enough to perceive this atmosphere electrified with suspicion and dread, crackling with bits and pieces of phantom elements thrown in between.

Something's wrong with this picture and I intend to find out why.

"Esme?"

Oh no! I forgot about Bill!

"Esme!"

"Coming!"

Her bare feet padding down the stairs as cautiously and silently as she conceivably can, Esme expected to find her husband in the living room or the dining room, only to discover that Bill is nowhere to be seen. Causing her to worry and call out:

"Bill! "Bill! Where are you?"

"In the kitchen!"

Breathing a sigh of relief, Esme creeped along to the kitchen, priding herself for being stealthy, when a male voice sang out to her:

"Hello, Honey!" Bill cheerily purred, kissing the back of her neck in a very passionate endearment before landing a kiss on her lips, clearly enjoying their rich sweet taste. Lately he had to admit he had grown addicted to having her around, something that scared him silly to know he can possess this kind of obsessive addiction.

"What's happening?"

"Oh, I just had a talk with myself, "Esme shrugged.

"And?" he teased with another lingering kiss.

"I decided that our marriage and you need me."

"Smart woman."

Esme bristled hastily and clandestinely at her husband's nonchalant praise of her without any other questions or concerns in regards to her talking to herself.by any facts alone, it seemed to her that Bill wasn't paying her any attention *at all*. For once, instead of being insulted, she was actually grateful.

Still…

How dare he! her wounded ego suddenly shrieked, coaxing her to bite back the *how dare you* down her throat, shooting sly dirty looks when he wasn't looking at her. Up to now, Esme could really feel her heart breaking into a truckload of teeny tiny pieces because she wanted him to ask her, to back her up, to support her… because she is his wife.

"What?"

"Nothing, Bill."

"Are you sure, Esme?"

"Yeah, I'm sure, why?"

"Because you look upset."

"I'm just tired. That's all. I did a lot of housework today."

It wasn't a total lie. She truly did a lot of housework today and she really is tired.

"Oh."

Oh…

One word, one lousy word was all it took for Esme to suck up all her outrage and discouragement as those two feelings crept around deep inside her fragmented heart.

"One little word."

"What, Esme?

"Nothing."

Nothing. How easy it is for one simple word to be brutally broken apart into two words. Nothing can easily remind her of her marriage to Bill should she believed him being accused of murder and attempted murder by a ghost who kind of remember how she exactly died!

Maybe she was being silly.

Maybe…

"Maybe."

"Hmm?'

"Oh, it's nothing."

Esme knew she was lying again. Then again, she also knew better than to start a fight with him only to end up bringing up sore wounds like Joanna and Amanda. Surely, they were the two coincidences bound together to Bill like twine wrapped around a package. All she had to do is to bring those two women up during a furious no-holds-barred blow up and…

No, she won't do it.

Not ever. "Penny for your thoughts?'

Esme smiled and shook her head enigmatically, her voice sad and wistful:

"It's too complicated and painful."

"Oh…okay."

Something in her tone stopped her, baffling her beyond any idea or recognition to speak of. She expected him to say more, ask her questions that would end up leading to the subjects of Joanna and Amanda. Questions that would go along to something, anything, bringing everything out to the open, saving their marriage or splintering it. How Esme really wanted to get this out so she can have some peace of mind in some way possible only to keep her mouth shut out of fear of learning the truth.

If there was such a truth…

"What happened to the Lilies of the Valley that were in a vase on the dining room table?"

"Oh no, not again," Bill growled, gently pulled away from her, his face crumpled in a grim setting around his lips and eyes.

"We're back to this *again*? Your imagination is getting too wild again. I already told you *I don't know*."

"No, not *those* Lilies of the Valley. These flowers were on the table yesterday."

"What flowers?"

Esme felt all the color flowing out of her face as her feverish mind blew itself up into overdrive, causing her to simply stare at him like he was stark-raving mad. Just like he's gawking at her right now.

Gaslighting her…

Oh my God, he's gaslighting me!

Still, she had to play dumb, play the part of a clueless wife who believed whatever her husband says.

With a moderate breath of a simple prayer, Esme tenderly asked again just to be perfectly clear:

"So, you have *never* seen the flowers? You have *never* put any flowers on the dining room table?"

"Once again no and no."

"Ever?"

"No."

His last answer was very firm and direct, putting Esme to the errant confines of her possible madness. With the attention of her delirium being within reach, she twirled away from her husband and ran up the stairs, two at a time, and over to where the locked bedroom door stood. With some bravery lurking in her heart and soul, she grasped the knob and turned it only to discover it rotating to open…and found nothing at all in the bedroom.

Not even the trunk.

"See? This room is ready for anything you want—including a nursery, Bill snapped, his face flushing and blushing completely.

"A nursery, Bill?" I'm confused…I thought you wanted to wait on children."

"When did I say this?"

"A couple of days ago."

"No, I didn't."

"But you did! You did!" Esme howled, her patience and sanity evidently wearing away to a kind of thinness she might not be able to get out of.

"Honey, do you feel okay?"

"Yes—no—I don't know. I really don't know," her voice cracked with so many emotions that Esme seemed to be on the verge of tears, her sudden attack of exhaustion now draining all her energy and feelings entirely.

Am I going crazy?

"Come on, you need some rest. If you aren't feeling any better, we will go to the doctor, okay?" Bill cooed as he gently wrapped his left arm tight around her shoulders, giving her a loving peck on her hair, the exact color of a raven's wing.

"But…but…" Esme stammered, longing to preserve the talking simply for the sake of expressing her rationalizations and reactions—thoughts and feelings, that is.

To him, her husband.

Just him…

"What's going on, Honey? Tell me."

"I don't know how to tell you. Something's off, Bill. I can *feel* it, but I can't *explain* it."

Walking around the small vacant room, her footsteps echoing and bouncing off the walls and floor, Esme grasped frantically for the answers she just couldn't or wasn't consented to go into detail with her husband, apart from the tiny bits of information she gave him as of now.

"Well, Esme?"

"Oh…leave me alone, Bill!"

She squealed those words at him as she ran away from him crying into her bedroom, slamming the door behind her before plopping herself on the bed, crying her eyes out until she fell fast asleep.

Eight

Esme dreamt about her twin sister's wine-colored journal glowing deep in the vast darkness between the two mattresses she is sleeping on. A strange dream, born from somewhere within the depths of her sleepy brain, one that didn't make any sense neither here nor there.

"Esme! Esme! Please wake up!"

An ice-cold hand forcefully gripped Esme's exposed left shoulder and shook it violently, making Esme growl and shake the hand off:

"Leave me alone!"

"Esme!"

Joanna sounded hurt, which pissed Esme off a little more than she had intended to.

"What? What do you want, Joanna? Because it is quite clear that I am going completely crazy since I can only feel and hear *you!*"

"What do you mean?"

"What do I mean? I feel and hear things that Bill doesn't feel and hear. I am sick and tired of being stuck between you two! So sick and tired of being stuck between deciding whether to tell Bill something or not! So sick and tired of being frightened for my life and suspecting Bill! *Ugh!* I don't even know what I am saying anymore!"

Boiling fresh tears fell down her ashen cheeks in a massive flood of hurt and despair onto her pillow that Joanna didn't have an answer for except to watch her younger sister helplessly. Suddenly

Esme sensed her madness going and growing uninhabited and in full force like wildflowers in a field. Esme honestly felt like she is going completely crazy at full throttle without braking

And all of this is breaking her heart…

"Esme, please talk to me."

"I can't, Joanna. Don't you see? I just can't and that's where it hurts the most."

Joanna's own phantom heart shattered for her younger sister's pain and torment yet at the same time it had come to all of this for the ghost to understand her own death in addition to how she died. Everything has its price and Esme's sanity had become the cost. A tough call, really, but one needed to survive this truth as well as to help her little sister survive exactly what Bill dishes out. Now more determined than ever, Joanna belted out:

"Yes, yes! You can, Esme! Now listen to me: we just have to survive all of this noise and slight of hand Bill is performing for his benefit and we will finally free!"

"But I don't *want* to be free, Joanna," Esme sniffled, rubbing her red, tear-stained eyes like a little child after being spanked. "I just want Bill to love me."

"Oh, Esme, that's not freedom. With him, it's a gilded prison and you have the key to get out. All you have to do is turn the key."

It's true even though Esme still hadn't had the strength to see it and know it…yet. Because it is easy to see the answers to Esme's predicament with clear eyes from the outside. On the other hand, it's harder to see the answers clearly from the inside and Esme is drowning intensely in her circumstances.

"Please, Joanna, just let me be! You never leave me alone! Leave me alone!"

"Never! You're my sister and you're in trouble! Even in danger! I won't always leave you alone until you are definitively safe and protected. Okay?"

"Okay."

The bone-deep chill that usually comes with Joanna's icy presence left as quickly as a gentle breeze, making the bedroom almost a little bit warmer than it was before. Plunging back into that much needed sleep, Esme bore this notion about being lost in the shadows.

The shadows…

The journal!

All of a sudden, waking up with an abrupt start, she shuddered violently as if dread is creeping and crawling home to stay while her eyes struggled to get into focus, gawking deep within the vast darkness now settling itself all over her bedroom.

"Hello?"

A massive stillness greeted and acknowledged her, its odd welcome brisk and bitter in its emphasis. Scared stiff if only for a mere second, Esme struggled once again to find her voice, its tone strangled and uneasy:

"Bill! Bill!"

This time, somewhere submerged in the shadows something heavy and dense swaggered and swayed freely throughout the darkness provided. One more time the faint-heartedness was within reach for Esme.

Bill should have been home by now! Where is he?

Esme's terrified mind screeched even as she blindly rushed over to where the light switch is located on the wall. Desperately slapping her hands all along and around the wall, fumbling to feel for a switch that is definitely here some place or another, before snapping it on as promptly as it could allow her to do so.

A creamy buttery yellow radiance swiftly dazzled and befuddled her, causing her to clumsily stumbled a bit in response. Darkness fled from her bedroom in terror as the light ruthlessly chased it away for an exaggerated moment in time. Esme had to admit that she was too frazzled to notice she wasn't alone. For over in the farthest corner of the bedroom, far away from the dazzlingly blinding brightness of her light-dazed eyes, stood a make figure dressed from head to foot in dark somber blackish gray patiently waiting for the right time to advance towards her.

Predator and prey…

Still blinded by the bright light, Esme didn't have the specific strength to see markedly, welcoming an opportunity for the man to noiselessly sneak up to her, hands outstretched almost in a comical manner had it not been for the scary fact that it is really happening and not in a nice way.

"Ahh!"

She managed a smothered scream as the man's strong gloved hands tightly clamped around her neck from behind, forcing her to fight desperately, frenziedly clawing at her neck while his hands continue to tensed their squeezing. Their owner's angry "ows" echoing through her head, thrown in between as he made headway to crush the life out of Esme until she blacked out or dies.

"Ow! You bitch!"

The man brutally threw Esme onto the floor as she dug her nails in deep, drawing blood and pain, not caring for her safety at all as she, barely conscious but still fighting for her life, dragged a sharp intense scratch burrowed in severely into his right hand from wrist to knuckle as her strength pulled the glove of his right hand, marking him to anyone else, including her as she tumbled into unconsciousness.

Once he had settled on her being out cold, he ran downstairs to create a chaotic flurry of sounds seemed to exploded all around the small house: faraway blast of glass shattering, heavy shuffling, and the awkward pounding of feet running along in the darkness followed by Bill's worried yell:

"Esme! Oh, Honey!"

His right hand thoroughly wrapped up from elbow to hand in a bleached white kitchen towel, Bill quickly grabbed and held her close to his chest, rocking her back and forth.

"Oh, Esme…Esme…Todd! Turn on the lights!"

With a flick of the switch, the bedroom was ablaze in creamy buttery light while Esme laid perfectly motionless in her husband's arms. Still in an insensible state, she was muttering something when Bill gingerly gathered her up and placed her on the rumpled bed covers with her head on the pillow. He kind of reckoned that as long as she didn't feel anything for the moment, she will be safe if Bill has his way. Snatching up both her icy hands, he rubbed them briskly, kissing them from time to time, his voice cracked and stressed anger and eagerness to get her back to life.

"Come on, Honey. Come on and wake up for me. Please, Honey."

"Why don't I call the ambulance and…"

"No! Todd, that won't be necessary."

Bill begged through clenched teeth and reckless agony, furiously possessive of his wife all at the same time from what Todd noted with a careful and suspicious eye. All at once, it reminded him of Joanna and her supposed heart attack. Supposed because Todd didn't believe that Joanna, who seemed to be in good condition, would end up dying from a cardiac arrest at the age of 33. Now Esme had been attacked and once again Mister Porcher refused help from those who could provide him with profession care.

"But Mister Porcher, she was found unconscious with nasty-looking scratch marks on her neck…"

"So."

"So? She's hurt!"

"It's manageable, Todd! It's not liked your sister and speaking of which, if you and your sister value living on this property and her job, then I would greatly suggest that you do as I say, hmm?"

Knowing that he was stuck between a rock and a hard place, but still worrying over Esme, Todd turned on his heel and walked out of the room without saying a single word to his sister's boss.

Meantime, Bill was torn between certain bouts of hugging her and shaking his wife from time to time. His voice hoarse with concern, he went on, determined to wake her up from this:

Wake up for me, Esme. Please, Honey."

He kept right on begging her, cajoling her to open her eyes and look at him as he continued to hug and shake her until he decided to give up for good if only for a little while. Exiting the bedroom, he shut the door with a soft click, unknowingly waking her up in the process.

"Bill…Bill?"

She muttered his name over and over again until she grew croaky without any hope or expectations. If she waited until tomorrow, Esme would have a better sense to talk to Bill once he gets home.

Her throat sore and hoarse, she folded herself over to her right side and into a little ball of a wounded human being. Falling fast asleep, she dreamt dreamless dreams.

Nine

Experiencing restlessness and intensity during her sleep, Esme chose to stick to slumbering with very little comfort to mainly her neck and right side of her face. Her throat still throbs acutely before finally and slowly easing into a dull pulsating ache every single time, she urged herself to swallow on impulsive cue, followed by a low husky "ow" bolting from her lips.

In the end, Esme completely possessed the chance to fall back to sleep and dream. Coming into a drawn focus, she dreamt of shadows with sprinkles of slotted spotty sunlight. Running into the hoped-for safety of the warm light, she tried her best to make sure to stay away from the fuzzy murkiness only to be strictly cut and fiercely scratched by ancient veiny hands who possess razor-sharp pointed fingernails. Scratches and cuts that drew buckets of blood as she struggled to live and be free. She almost succeeded when a sharpened wooden stake shot out from the obscurities.

"No!"

Esme screamed at the top of her lungs as the stake furiously impaled her, waking her up as a result. Hurriedly, she snapped open her eyes over a crack, expecting an angry glare of the bedroom light welcoming and chiding her back from the land of the unconsciousness. Deprived of any reservation, Esme was surprised to find the luminosity switched off, nothing but the brilliant ashy yellow sunshine shining off the walls. Wincing obviously, she smiled a sickly smile at the odd idea of surviving another day after what happened to her.

Wait a minute…what really happened to me?

"You were attacked," Joanna piped up, concerned about her younger sister's health and safety.

"I was? By who?"

They were questions now bugging her right at this very moment. For the time being, Esme couldn't understand what actually took place with her save a sore throat as a result.

What turned up last night that it ended up with me getting a sore throat?

"Guess."

"No…not Bill…"

"Honey…"

"Bill! Oh, Bill…" she wailed as a pair of strong arms gently wrap themselves around her, comforting her in the darkness.

"Shh…shh…I'm here, Honey."

Bill's soothing voice broke through her foggy train of pain and thought like a plow tilling the soil, his warm hand softly stroking her hair, making her fall back to sleep.

Certain that Esme has fallen back into a deep sleep, Bill slipped out of the bed to stand beside it, taking the advantage to address the ghost he knew was in the room.

"You still here, Joanna? Listen to what I have to say regarding you little sister. You thought you would win, eh? Well, it looks like I am going to win as far as Esme is concerned. As for Esme, she will *never* know who I am for as long as she lives. I am through with you."

Confident and brash, Bill shoved his left hand in his pocket, digging and mixing the dried herbal concoction of dill, lavender, and oregano until he felt it was ready. Seizing a handful of this jumble, he began to scatter all over the floor, at the doorway, around the bed, at the closet, inside the closet, and on the window sill, chanting in a singsong voice:

"In my hand, these are the herbs of triumph for me, a losing battle for Joanna Teresa Porcher. In my hand, I cut off Esme Leona Porcher off from Joanna's influence. In my hand…ugh!"

The deep scratches on his right hand from knuckles to forearm began to itch and rudely interfere with his spell, fully unaware that his spell and the herbs themselves were defective just by the prickling and smarting. These deep cuts, coming from the "attempt" to smash open the window, practically impaired the spell before he could even finish it.

Three long scratches in all…

"Get out of here, Joanna! You're no longer welcomed here!"

As if on cue, a soft fluttery breeze skittered in before turning into a mini whirlwind scattering all the herbal hodgepodge from one end of the room to the other, dusting the mixture into a fine annoying mess all over the place.

But Bill didn't mind.

"That's better," he purred as he watched the chaotic mishmash ultimately settled down on the floor. Once everything is calmed down, he said to himself:

"Now to check on my Esme…"

My Esme.

Lingering in those two words, happy as a proverbial clam, Bill stalked up to Esme's bed, staring contently at her as she slept. Reaching down, he took his time stroking her hair, watching for any signs of distress or restlessness, things he might be concerned over. When he didn't see anything to burden himself about, he breathed a sigh of relief before leaving his wife to her rest. Closing the door with a quiet yet satisfying click, he felt comfortable enough to go downstairs and tend to his wounds before sleeping on the couch for another night.

To all appearances, Esme's room gave the impression of being absolutely calmed and free from the upcoming disturbance. A couple of minutes later, a window compulsively flew open and was followed by a fresh burst of crisp cool air scooting about like an ethereal being moving around.

"Joanna…Joanna, please help me…"

Teetering between consciousness and unconsciousness, Esme's weak voice, scratchy and gravelly, moaned for her older sister to come back to her, her fear forcing her heart to have some pretty fierce palpitations, even in her obscure slumber.

"Joanna…"

As if on cue, Joanna vigilantly approached her younger sister's bed without any hesitation. Being asleep, Esme barely noticed the abrupt drop of temperature much less open her eyes to finally see and focus on the ghostly face of her older sister drifting in the air. Still there was endless amounts of different frames of mind and emotions running rampant, not for Esme, but for Bill himself.

"I'm right here, Esme," Joanna gently soothed, her voice as kind and caring as always.

"Joanna! You're still here!"

"Shh! You will wake up Bill!"

"But you're here, Joanna…I was so afraid that Bill had gotten rid of you."

Joanna lightly placed an icy cold hand on Esme's feverish forehead, soothing away all the worries, the terrors, and the nightmares that plagued her younger sister almost endlessly. Yet at her older sister's chilly touch, Esme regained her composure during her sleep once again. She was about to do more for, even say more to Esme, when Joanna heard the tell-tale stomping of Bill's steps giving himself away to the spectral woman before it's too late.

Try as he may, Bill accidentally made the bedroom yawned a bit too loud, forcing him to flinch at the prolonged squeal of the hinges not used to being opened at breakneck speed when it has been open at any speed all the time. Acting on impulse and fear, he marched around the bedroom without bothering to concern himself regarding Esme and her sleep despite the noticeable fact that she was dead asleep, much to Bill's relief. Slamming the window shut without any thought or regards as to why it was ajar in the first place. He nodded to himself in great satisfaction at controlling the ins and outs of those crossing the threshold of Esme's room, whispering childishly:

"No one comes in and out of this room unless it is by my permission."

Once more, completely confident in his power to banish the ghost of his late wife, Bill lumbered out of the door and somewhat clacked it shut, causing Joanna to emerge from the shadows and to float up to Esme's bedside.

"Esme…Esme! Please wake up!"

Mumbling something inaudible, Esme flipped onto her left side, her sleep amazingly still undisturbed, an astonishing feat in itself.

"Esme, please wake up…please!"

"No."

"Esme!"

"No, I say…"

"Ugh!"

The only good thing about being a ghost is that Time is not important. In Joanna's case, she may have all the Time in the world while in Esme's circumstance, it didn't. in Joanna's choice of opinion, Esme deserves to have all the Time in the world, to live until she becomes a very old woman.

Not like her…

"Esme!"

"What?"

"You need to get up! You need to leave Bill right now before it's too late! So you can live a long and happy life."

"But I already have a long and happy life with Bill," Esme reasoned with a slight wail.

"No, you don't!"

Annoyance prickled at the back of Joanna's mind as she tried not to be as loud as she really wanted to be. Oh, how she truly wanted to *shake* Esme for being so damn stubborn and mousy.

With clenched teeth, Joanna abruptly grabbed her younger sister by her left shoulder and roughly shook it as hard as she could without making the bed springs betray their creak in loud protest, even if only for a little bit, forcing the ethereal lady to flinch a tiny bit more than she wanted to. As a matter of fact, she was extremely expecting Bill to crash through the bedroom door at any moment.

"Damn it! Esme!"

Ten

Bill's head split open and bore nightmare about his Esme. About her stumbling and running away from him after finding out who and what he is accurately. Scampering away from him, screaming franticly in horror as he chased after her without a care in the world, a piece of paper clenched tightly in his right hand, she hid and there from time to time, frustrating him right to the core. Joanna jumping in front of him, in full corporal form, blocking his way, her voice a witchy screech as she taunted him:

"You will never kill her for sacrificial money, Bill! Give it and her up!"

"Damn it, Joanna! Why don't you stay dead and let me have my Esme!" he shouted to the treetops at his late wife, who is smiling serenely at him, her teasing developing into a ruthless taunt:

"No because she is not your *Esme!"*

"Yes, she is!"

"Do you love her?"

"Yes."

"Then why can't you turn yourself in for the crime you committed against me and save her from a certain death?"

"Because it is not that easy…"

"There were more, isn't it?"

He didn't have to say a thing since his silence yelled out his guilt to her, making Joanna bristle at him cruelly and furiously starved of any words, but generating enough heat for Bill to feel her vicious emotions against him. Seeking to find some kind of solace from his late wife, he chooses to plea for her humanity and love for him to let him be:

"I didn't do anything to make you die."

"Excuse me? You know that it is not true."

"It *is* true! It's *my truth*!" Bill bellowed at the top of his lungs before grumbling, "It is my truth." Rubbing his eyes so very heard in order to attempt to get rid of this unwelcomed vision of Joanna, he woke up seeing stars behind his eyelids.

"Shit…Esme."

Jumping off the couch like his butt was in fire, stumbling and crashing into Esme's room, Bill was absolutely breathless with total fear. His eyes caught the sight of his wife lying in bed, undisturbed and in complete phases of restless slumber. Being ever so cautious, he crept up to Esme's bed, his eyes never wavering, his hands self-ish to touch her as he gently stroked her flyaway wayward hair in mini-strokes for minutes at a time.

"Bill?" she babbled from out of the blue.

His hand became deathly motionless, his voice trembling with reluctance and exhilaration:

"Yes, Honey?"

"I had a dream about Joanna. She wanted to save me from you."

"Oh, Esme…"

Disappointment and sadness stole into his heart as he watched her fall back fast asleep, fully relaxed and perfectly unaware of what she said to him. At the same time Bill felt a true sense of outright betrayal by his herbal banishment spell as well as by Joanna herself.

She's back! Joanna's really back, damn it!

His mind shrieked at him even as he recognized himself as being off-balanced and desperate. More than anything, despite Esme clearly being the wrong choice for him as he knows now, he certainly wanted Joanna to get out of their lives and stop influenc-ing Esme into leaving him, thus, taking his wife away from him.

Joanna, he determined now more than ever, has to go…

"Esme! Wake up! Honey, why does Joanna want to save you from me?"

"Good God, Bill…just let her sleep until we are ready to do what we plan to do with her."

"Amanda! What are you doing here? You're supposed to be at home, *acting* like you're recovering from a suicide attempt." Bill seethed, grabbing Amanda by her arms a started to push her out of the bedroom door, but to his dismay, she proved that she was still stronger than him physically.

"I got bored and miss my Bill so very much," she pouted, her fingers seductively walking up his chest, her arms creeping up to wrap themselves around his neck like a vine.

With a boyish smirk, he gave her a quick peck on her lips, Bill touched his forehead to hers in a loving gesture, his voice beguiling and deep:

"Amanda, Honey, I need you to go home. I haven't forgotten our plan but I need time. Okay?"

"Okay."

"Good girl. I will see you later."

"Promise?"

"Promise."

" Give me a kiss," she demanded, not moving an inch until she gets her wish granted.

"With my wife around?" he asked, trying to stifle a laugh while striving to sound shocked.

"Silly Billy, she's asleep."

"Oh. Amanda, what am I going to do with you?"

"Keep your promises, shut up, and kiss me."

"That's all?"

"That's all."

Bill smiled sweetly as he allowed Amanda to pull his head down towards hers, his lips warm, passionate, and inviting as Amanda responded and kissed him in kind.

"Okay, you got your kiss, now go," Bill growled playfully, slapping her flirtatiously on the butt to get his lover moving before going back into the bedroom to play the dutiful and attentive husband.

DECAY OF SORROW

Sitting ever so silently and patiently by Esme's side, Bill waited for his wife to wake up, to answer him while not allowing Joanna to come near his wife ever again. A fruitless cause, he knew, of course but one he must strain to implement.

Never again will Joanna tell *his wife* these nasty lies about him *ever…*

"There's no way in Hell that Esme will be taken from me by some damned ghost!" Bill drawled and spat under his breath, his hands thoughtlessly opening and closing into tight angry fists even as he continued to watch his wife sleeping peacefully and innocently as a child. Rage grew and swelled deep in his heart; a certain case of unreasonableness controlled his gullible mind.

"How dare Joanna! Trying to take you away from me!" he barked and grounded out a bit too loudly, the last words borne from his intense hatred of Joanna and her supernatural sway she held over her younger sister.

Deprived of any warning, Bill graspingly clamped his large hands tight around Esme's small slim neck, his rough fingers firmly pressing themselves deep into the silky softness her skin provides. From the unyielding squeeze of his hands around her neck, her struggle to breathe so painfully obvious to endure, waking Esme up in the process. Struggling to wrangle herself free with all her might, her voice cracking and croaking with a great effort to breathe from Bill's super strong clutches.

"Bi—ll…Bi—ll…"

With all her determined strength in battling for her life against Bill's ever tightening wringing, Esme frenziedly kicked, punched, and even scratched her way to her freedom, going so far as to angrily kneed him in the nuts, an act that caused him to yelped out in intense tenderized agony and fell to the floor, rolling about and gently cradling the injured area quite gingerly, breathless and crying in extreme suffering. Tackling to get away from him, Esme thought she was free and clear out of Bill's grasp when he managed to snatched up her left ankle in a bruising grip, coercing her to yowl at the top of her lungs, kicking out and away at his hand with her right foot in swift brutal kicks.

"Esme! Ow! Damn It, Esme!" he gasped as he tried to thwart the foot blows quite weakly and miserably.

"Get away from me! Go away and stay away from me!" she croaked-screamed, stumbling and tumbling her way into the bathroom, slamming the door shut and locking it with one quick twist of her wrist. Her neck and left ankle betrayed the fresh revealing signs of bruising, throbbing and sore, caught by the mirror's eagle eye as she looked around for something and yet nothing. Dazed and confused, she huddled behind the sink, tears of horror and anguish gushing down her heated cheeks as she bawled her heart out.

"Esme…"

In spite of his raging intense sensitive discomfort, Bill painstakingly collapsed on his hands and knees, his nuts thumping a severe painful sensation tattoo, a heavy fog looming deep inside his uncertain head slowly displaced itself almost straight away. Bringing about this increased fear that he did something wrong to her, he dragged his wounded self over to the bathroom door, knocking and slapping faintly on its polished wood, his voice hoarse and broken.

"Esme? Honey, please open this door. It's me."

The pause for his wife's answer seemed to be too long, lasting for minutes then forever, making him both very nervous and anxious to a fault. Usually in the short pleasant moments of their marriage, Esme would have responded swiftly back to him whenever they have a conversation. Now with his stomach tied up in awfully bad taut contortions, those knot constrictions choking and restraining with each and every twist, making him feel left out of his wife's love and good graces all of a sudden.

Short of notice…

Starved of touch…

Deprived of hope.

"Esme? Honey…"

"No."

Hurriedly and with some trouble, Bill wriggled to sit up in disapproval of his nuts searing in fierce soreness, his sitting position forcing him to wince noticeably in distress and confusion. Of course, he sadly had to say that he knew what he did to her, that was utterly clear, but what if he acts like he didn't know? That his mind went blank when he attacked her? Like he blacked out or something close to it? He pulled off that "I didn't know how it happened" stunt with Joanna and Amanda during their disagreements, fights, and even Joanna's death and Amanda's hypothetical morbid effort, but Esme was—is—different from those two women as well as the others who have crossed his path:

She had actually *survived* his assault....

"Esme...Honey...I'm sorry."

He listened in pained silence for her to reply, waiting to see if she would change for him if he didn't pay attention to the dangerous crazes that crawl about deep inside his muddled head and rotting soul. For Bill was something of a serial killer dressed in normal skin and normal clothes while he searched for the next sacrificial cow to gain money from in the form of insurance money and death.

Only Amanda doesn't have an insurance policy on her.

Too bad.

She is and was such a great sex partner....

"You *strangled* me! You could have *killed* me, you know?"

She squawked, her high voice growing stronger yet betraying the possible everlasting or brief effects of her strangulation.

"Yes, I know. I didn't mean it."

Liar, his inner voice scolded him, for he recognized himself as a liar, a stealer of life, a vicious individual while a stillness followed him, this strong sense of quietness that nearly frightened the Hell right out of him as this faint hush emerged from the bathroom to sweep all through the house. In his opinion, his wife's motionlessness was something to be terrified about, his mind running into overdrive to figure out how to win her, understand her, and even love her. To win her love for him and good graces back.

"Esme?"

"Go away."

Suffering both from the rejection and discouragement, Bill took his dear sweet time picking himself up off the floor, the pain between his legs throbbing into a mutable hum, and limped noticeably down the stairs towards the living room. Sinking down into the plush luxuries of his soft couch with an aggrieved long-winded sigh, he complied to delicately parked himself inaudibly in the gloom and the shadows up until it was almost unbearable and even then, he continued to sit and simmer deep the lightlessness swept all around him.

In the meantime, Esme unquestionably made sure that the bathroom is locked, her anxiety pulsing and sizzling hidden inside her heart and soul even as she cracked open the bathroom window.

"God, I need a hot bath," she stammered, staggering over to the bathtub. Turning on the hot and cold taps together, her hands and body still shaking, Esme managed to build a certain peacefulness in the bustling blast of rushing water filing up the empty tub. She took her time to delicately strip off her clothes while in the short term, ignoring the sharp pricks and hurts of discomfort in addition to the growing dark purplish-blue discolorations, displayed by the floor-length mirror attached to the bathroom door, wrapped around her neck and ankle ever so definitely.

The water is stinging and alive with warmth as Esme smoothly and thoughtfully lowered her tired achy body into the wonderfully heated water. Her entire body unfurled agreeably in bits and stretches deep within the tub's adequate space, its steam lightly fondling her skin and face like an otherworldly lover's caresses, making her both sleepy and feeling safe.

"Esme?"

"Go away, Bill…wait, *Joanna*?"

"Of course. Good God, what happened to your neck and ankle?"

"Oh, that…Bill did it."

"What?"

"Shh! Not too loud, okay? We don't want Bill to come crashing in here through the door, do you?"

Although she couldn't *see* her older sister, Esme had the knowledge of Joanna's closeness, giving the younger sister enough safety and comfort from this moment on. Her voice worried and tense, Joanna pleaded:

"Esme, please listen to me. You have to leave him! Look at your neck and ankle!"

Seething inside, Joanna's icy fingers went about poking and touching her younger sister's neck and ankle with great care, a deepest concern, and a motherly compassion.

"Esme..."

"I heard you, Joanna. But how?" she dragged out, exhausted, lost, and all alone in this trap.

"We have to think about it and plan it, okay?" Joanna replied, her mind spinning at high speed to find answers and help for Esme and her predicament.

"I hope very soon."

"Me too, Esme, me too."

Hours passed until the water grew quite chilly to the point of making Esme's teeth chattering, her skin all goose pimply, and her body shivering. Lucky for Esme always made sure to have a fresh pair of underwear to accompany her pajamas here in the bathroom. Dressed her pajamas, feeling fresh and clean, she dashed into her bedroom, locked the door her, shutting Bill out once and for all, if only for the night. Finally feeling safe and secure against Bill with her locked door, Esme experienced some peace of mind.

Eleven

Bill ran smack dab into a brick wall of anger and failure, making him fell shut out and punished as a result. As he slept, the pain between his legs dulled itself into a light drone of tenderness while dreaming of Joanna rising from the grave, wrathfully demanding on how he could hurt Esme that way like some Goddess of Justice descending upon her followers who just happened to displease her. In his dream, Bill sensed as though he had steel wool cutting intensely in his mouth, making his mouth bleed from the pressure and abrasiveness. In his dream, Joanna was really flesh and blood and totally pissed off, no longer a ghost, poking and prodding him with a tree stick that looked like a small branch only to turn out to be a broomstick.

"Answer me. Why did you hurt Esme? If she's your Esme, why did you hurt her neck and ankle, you bastard!"

"Mmph!" he grumbled, tears of pain streaming down his hot cheeks as Joanna angrily poked and slapped him with the broomstick over and over again, repeating her questions with such frequency and frantically as if she was on repeat. Waking up with a start, Bill's mouth felt dry and raw instead of the bloodied harsh penetrating coils that seemed to be cruel punitive measures in his opinion. A great heap of anxiety overwhelmed him suddenly and without any mercy, leaving him shaken and broken all at once.

"Esme…"

He stumbled up the stairs over to Esme's bedroom door, his large sweaty hands clumsily grabbing the door knob with little success in opening the door. Add to the fact that the door is locked despite his desperation in turning the knob. Disappointed, Bill turned around and went back down to his couch, sitting there in a dejected state.

He strongly and unexpectedly yearned for Esme now more than anything, crave her with such passion and intensity that the destroyer in him instantaneously pines for her destruction right now while a tiny bit of him really wished she remained like she was a week or so ago: loving and trusting. On the other hand, the way he treated her just now already told him that it would be a slim chance in Hell she intends to ever love him again.

"Oh, Esme…"

His head in his hands, Bill mourned in low tones the instant death of his young marriage only for a few seconds before a vicious defiant fury seared a fiery hole deep in the crushed spaces of his depraved heart.

So, she wants out? Over her dead body!

A fluffy melodic tone coming from his cell phone instantly remind him of his broken promise to Amanda as he reached over to grab the phone off the coffee table, causing him to pause ever so slightly. Stopping to notice the bright arrival of the dawn slowly crawling into his home. Looking at his phone once again, he winced and kicked himself at how he had forgotten his previous engagement with Amanda. Pressing the green phone on his screen, his voice sounded wearier and more exhausted than he intended to be.

"Hello. Amanda? I can explain—"

"Where the hell were you last night?" Amanda snarled into his ear, forcing Bill to grimace a tiny bit more than he should have and wanted.

Walking on eggshells at present, he sauntered over to the dining room table, his cell phone nearly glued to his ear as he constructed some kind of security in keeping his conversation with Amanda out of Esme's earshot. It was enough for him to smile a feral cruel unflattering smirk that looked more like an arrogant sneer. A creepy smirk trailed by a brilliant flash of deep-seated anger dancing like a flame in his eyes, urging him to snap:

"I almost killed her last night."

Silence shadowed Amanda's side of the phone before she asked in an apprehensive pitch:

"Who?"

"Esme. She tried to leave me and so I tried to strangle her."

He knew that it was a partial lie, but it worked because Amanda asked:

"*What*? Is she okay?"

Sneering at the sincere concern in Amanda's words, Bill tried to tone down his anger and smugness as he replied:

"I think she is. She's locked up in her room right now."

"Are you sure?"

"Of course, I'm sure."

"Are you still coming over?" Amanda inquired after being hesitant for a little while.

"Yes."

"What are you going to do? With her, I mean."

"Oh, I'll fix her. Believe me, I'll fix her,"

"Bill! You 're not going to try to kill her again, are you?"

"No, of course not! I need her to realize that I'm the best thing that has ever happened to her and then she had no choice but to stay with me."

A hurt silence fell on Amanda's part, twisting the knife deeper into her now broken heart as her ears caught the hopeful glee in his voice, her own voice brittle and pained:

"But…what about us? Don't you want me to stay with you instead of her?"

Oh, shit, his mind screeched, slamming on the brakes, *Amanda! I had forgotten about Amanda!*

Clearing his throat, Bill made sure that he sounded loving, contrite, and sincere.

"I'm sorry, Amanda. I just got all caught up in my role as this loving husband."

"It's all right, Bill. But are you sure you aren't falling in love with Esme? And isn't that *not* the wisest thing to do?"

She didn't know what she is saying, her broken heart was already yelling those words to him even though she spoke these same words in a softer tone.

"Yes, of course. But we do need Esme's signature on the insurance forms, right?"

"Right."

"What?"

"Nothing, Bill. When will I see you?"

"I told you I will…"

"When?"

"Soon."

"Just checking. See you soon?"

"Okay."

He hung up, got up, and wandered over to the kitchen window…

It was the bright creamy buttery yellow sunlight that woke Esme up with a start when it struck her right in the closed eyelids. Moaning out in annoyance, she flipped herself onto her stomach and strained to will herself back to sleep. The next thing to blindside her senses is the mouthwatering aroma of bacon and eggs being cooked to delicious perfection. This bombardment, including the cheery sunshine, was more than enough to keep her wide awake for the day.

"Mmm…"

Esme's stomach growled in response to the fresh sizzling sounds and salty smells of bacon and its grease cooking. By all means, it could be just her imagination, but these aromas seem so real and savory.

"I guess I better get up."

She grumbled a wee bit as she struggled to get herself into a comfortable sitting position. Hair scattered all over her head, Esme looked like some partied out partier who went one binge too many. It would have been hilarious had it not been for the dark purplish-blue fingermarks wrapped around her hoggishly around her neck and left ankle.

A faint knock on the bedroom door, followed by Bill's tentative pitch:

"Esme, breakfast is ready and I'm going to work."

"Okay…"

She waited a couple of minutes or so to confirm that Bill really went to work as promised. That way she was absolutely certain before leaving the bedroom. Tip toeing down the stairs and into the kitchen, Esme could smell the faint salty traces of cooked bacon mingled with the prepared freshness of eggs. Peering carefully around for any possible sign of her husband, completely satisfied with his absence, she cautiously sat herself down at the head of the dining room table as if the table was going to bite her. With great relish, she dug in and enjoyed her breakfast sitting before her like some starving fiend. Over to her right stood a good-sized glass of orange juice to accompany her scrambled eggs, two strips of bacon, and two pieces of wheat toast.

Everything she wanted for breakfast, mundane as it seems….

"Mmm," Esme declared again, hungrily savoring each and every forkful like someone who is literally starving for food. Delicious as it was the tasty saltiness of her bacon forcing her tastebuds to beg for some orange juice. Reaching out for her glass, she sipped it down in ten cautious sips.

"Oh, my…yuck…too sweet…"

She flinched and screwed up her face at how unpleasantly and sickly sweet her orange juice tasted. If hindsight was 20/20, she would have taken a sip instead of ten. Without thinking, she poured the rest of the orange juice down the drain.

Out of trusting Bill…

"Bill…did Bill do this? To me?"

At such a thought of Bill possibly have the balls to, by any chance, poison her, her stomach swayed and turned, flipping and flopping so violently that it made her feel like throwing up at any minute. Grabbing a clean glass, Esme filled it with water and gulped it down without rinsing her mouth out as fast as she can. Until she almost choked. She didn't care just as long as she get that damned unpleasantly sickly-sweet taste out of her mouth.

"Ugh! Oh God!"

Darting up the stairs and to the bathroom, Esme bowed over the toilet, the damned super sugary taste adhered to her tastebuds and mouth like some sole survivor of a shipwreck clinging to a life raft and threw up everything that was in her stomach, including her once delicious breakfast. Snatching up a bottle of mouthwash, she swilled until that nasty taste became a bad memory, her breath minty fresh.

"Esme! I'm home…Esme?"

Oh crap…he's home already? Oh no, not again…

"Esme!"

Bill caught her bent over the porcelain toilet bowl, pale, sweaty, and sickly-looking once again. On the sink stood a half full bottle of minty green mouthwash, ready for use.

"Oh, Esme…"

"Hi, Bill. How was work?" she whispered before falling down in a dead faint.

Twelve

Sluggishly waking up from her knocked out sleep, groggy and yet totally reinvigorated as far as snoozing goes. Her stomach still a bit queasy and topsy turvy, Esme took great care in getting out of the bed. Her only complaint is that her head is pounding a mile a minute, the pain intense and ugly to its core.

"Oh my," she slurred inaudibly just before her stomach commanded to go back to the bathroom so she can empty it violently. The action hurt her abdominal muscles and head so much that she kept on heaving till she retched no more.

"Oh my," she weakly repeated before making any effort to move on her hands and knees at a snail's pace back to her bed, her room. She almost made it when her older sister's cry of alarm broke through the thick fuzziness clogging her head, forcing her to cower in tortured distress.

"Esme! What the hell do you think you're doing? Where are you going?"

"Bed…my bed," Esme sobbed, her eyes burning with tears, not realizing she is lying on the floor, merely a few feet from her opened bedroom door. Shivering and exhausted to the bone, she curled herself up into a ball and whimpered out her pain-filled discouragement.

"No…"

She didn't even bother to fight or struggle when Bill silently walked up behind her, picked her up gently and lovingly, and carried her weak body back to her room, compassionately placing her down on the bed as if she was a precious package.

"Just lay there and rest. I will bring you some hot tea, okay?"

"Okay. Just make sure that the tea's not too sweet like the orange juice. That's why I got sick."

"Oh…okay…"

Closing her eyes to her husband and that damned worried look resting on his face, Esme gingerly wished herself back to sleep while Bill went downstairs to prepare a cup of tea for her. Sleeping just for the sake of having dreamless dreams for once, Esme simply allowed the darkness to swallow her up whole, letting her snooze fitfully. From time to time her drowsy ears caught a click of the door here and a clink of dishware there, oddly comforting sounds to make her sleep better. Less tossing and turning for her part, but enough to put her back into a deep sleep.

"Esme."

She jumped up suddenly, sitting ramrod stiff in her bed with unfocused eyes fruitlessly scanning every inch of her gloomy-looking room even though she was still stuck in dreamless slumber, her wide-awake ears captured the rapid thumping of her wildly frightened heart. For a moment there, Esme didn't know where she was or how she got there, startling her into fight mode, arms and hands and legs and feet flailing and slapping and kicking in all directions.

"Ow—*ow*! Esme, stop kicking and hitting me! You're safe!"

Bill's yelps of pain and frustration eventually reached Esme's ears, waking her up from her drowsy trance only to find herself with her arms clamped down into the mattress by her side, thanks to his vice-like bruising grip.

"What happened?"

"You were in a daze and attacked me!" he seethed, gingerly taking his hands off her arms as guardedly as he conceivably can. She frowned at him, obviously insulted by his actions towards her. Nevertheless, she held in reserve her voice, which sounded contrite and sincere:

"I'm sorry."

He didn't say anything at all except he lightly positioned his right hand on her right cheek in a loving forgiving caress. Her eyes and face betrayed their pleasure at being touched like this by him simply by lighting up in a happy glow as she welcomed this tender display of affection. Even in her sickness, she had to come clean she still needed her husband around now more than ever, hoping against hope he would change for her so that she wouldn't have to leave him at all.

Somewhere inside this bedroom, there was this faint moan of utter disappointment coming from out of nowhere. Joanna's lament. Upon hearing this, hiding his surprise and knowledge, Bill simply smiled to himself as he hugged his Esme possessively to him.

He had just won without having to redo the herbal spell to banish his late wife.

"All right, Honey. You need some rest, okay? I'll fix you some chicken noodle soup for dinner, hmm?"

"Homemade or from a can?"

"Homemade, of course."

"Okay."

He chuckled, smiling a genuine smile at her as he kissed her tenderly on the lips.

It worked! My lie really worked! Now I can have Esme all to myself! Take that, Joanna!

"Now you must rest," Bill commanded with a quick buss on her forehead before leaving her lying on the bed in a state of blissful rest.

Slowly closing the door behind him with a soft click, Bill pilled out his cell phone and dialed a number without stopping to think about it.

"Hello?"

"Amanda?"

"Oh, it's you. What do you want?"

"You," Bill purred right into the phone, hoping that Amanda will make it easier to him.

"What about Esme?"

"What about her?"

"Did you really choose me over her?"

"Yes.'

'Are you going to get rid of her soon?"

As soon as possible."

Thirteen

Esme slept for a little bit longer than Bill expected. Truth be told when he added a splash of anti-freeze to her glass of orange juice, he hadn't foreseen just how very sick she would eventually become. Not that he minds her sleeping in bed for hours; in fact, he was quite happy to see that she is still asleep. Besides, he really wasn't ready to cook soup right now.

Right now, he must look ion on Esme…

Like clockwork, he checked in on her, exhaustively assured and happy with his wife's sleeping arrangements and comfort and such. The only thing he didn't consider comfortable or even satisfied with was how he was going to conceal Esme from Amanda and vice versa without the two women encountering each other if only for a little while longer. he tried it once upon a time and was successful in the execution of the plan, but he had any name and another life back then.

Brooding wistfully, Bill grimaced as he found his mind casually drifting backwards to the ritual he enjoyed performing: stealing a new name off from the obituaries, move to a new city or town where no one knows him at all, find a woman he could marry, and have her sign the insurance documents, live here in town or in the city for a year or so—that is, if he's lucky—have her end up in a fatal accident or sudden death from an "illness", collect the money, get the hell out of Dodge, and go on finding the next mark. By all means necessary, it was wrong of him to pick and get hitched to his late wife's sister; up to now it was always too taboo for him to do such a thing, but he couldn't help himself with Esme, he guessed.

Still, he prided himself on how he juggled and handled more than one woman without getting caught.

Yet.

With a full determination to *not* get ensnared in his own game, Bill wished he could throttle Joanna for butting in and trying to destroy his plans for his own greedy money-making ways, forever banishing her from this world in return.

"Joanna."

His ears perked up and made out Esme's muttering of her older sister's name, causing him to go back to the bed and lean over to check if she was really asleep. Once he determined that she really was out like a light, he was about to leave the bedroom once more when he heard Esme's whisper drifting from the covers and out into the suddenly slightly chilled air:

"Joanna."

Fury unexpectedly exploded inside the depths of his head and heart like two bombs detonating, driving Bill to growl into Esme's ear out spitefulness and hurt, "Joanna's gone for good. She left this world and won't ever come back. *Ever.*"

"No!"

"Yes!"

"No…no…no…"

She sobbed shrilly and weakly, her tears rolling scorching and steady onto her pillow. Perversely satisfied, he sauntered out of the bedroom, leaving her to cry her heart out in her fidgety slumber.

But did Joanna really leave?

A convulsion rustled deep through his bones in consideration of an intense chill burrowing its razor-sharp talons into him, ripping and piercing into his vulnerable belly. What this chill is, Bill didn't know or couldn't fathomed, much less cared at a split second. Just something that may or may not be supernatural.

Still…

"Joanna?"

His mind in a frantic spiral, his voice fractured only a tad as his icy blue stare frantically scanned to the room for a ghost who wouldn't show up for him anyways.

"Coward!" he spat under his breath into the frosty air, shivering aggressively against the freezing drop of temperature here in the room, the icy chill swirling here and there from all corners of the room. An angry cold borne out of ferocity, exasperation, and wretchedness aimed directly at him.

"What do you want, Joanna? *Her?* Too bad because Esme is mine. Do you hear me? *Mine! I* won! *You* lost! Get over it!"

Bill laughed manically at the cold air swirling all around him, blowing about like a tornado as it tried its best to knock him down. Struggling and screaming with crazed laughter, shocked that Esme is still_snoozing in the midst of the chaos, Bill grew defiant and cruel, teeth bared, a junkyard dog howling at the moon.

In response, the mini tornado brutally pushed and shoved Bill out of the bedroom, slamming the door shut.

"Joanna?" Esme squeaked, waking up to the door smashing itself closed and a noiseless tranquil room. "Joanna?"

Icy cold hands gingerly gripped Esme's hands, securely squeezing them as an answer, telling the younger sister wordlessly that her older sister is here.

"Shh…it's okay. You're safe with me here."

"I'm safe…I'm safe…"

Esme tumbled back to sleep, fully content in her safe little world while peacefully dreaming of Joanna drifting back and forth like a ghostly sentinel, looking for something yet finding nothing at all, much to Joanna's anxiety. The house is well lit, giving it a benevolent and cozy appearance by nature despite having nothing in each room. Its walls are beautifully decorated in warm sunshiny yellows, rich creams, and strangely cheery cherry woods. A curious combination to be sure, but one that managed to truly work in their own ways.

Yeah, she would totally live in this house…

"Hello?" Esme called out, startled to discover how her voice didn't echoed and bounced off the walls and floors. Even her own footfalls were hushed with every step she makes.

"Hello? Joanna?"

"Hello!" replied a female voice, cheery and welcoming as well as sounding a bit familiar just like this house, inviting Esme to go on this strange little hunt for her older sister.

"Where are you?"

"Over here, Esme."

Standing in the middle of one of the rooms is a tall beautiful woman with shoulder-length raven hair, olive skin, and sparkling topaz eyes, her smile is as warm as the sun.

"Joanna!"

"Hello, little sister."

"What? How?"

"I can only be seen in corporeal—or bodily—form by you in your dreams," Joanna explained with a simple wave of her left hand.

"Can I see you outside of my dreams from now on?" Esme asked, hope dancing in her voice and heart.

"Unfortunately, no. only in your dreams."

"Oh—okay," Esme expressed her total disappointment in this knowledge.

"Look, I don't have much time in your dream, but you're in danger. Your orange juice is poisoned by Bill."

"No! Why?"

"Because he doesn't want to lose you *and* you're getting too close to what he doesn't want you to know. What it is, I don't know."

Esme wanted so much to protest all the facts being thrown at her right now only to knew that they were true deep in her faintly beating heart. The too sweet orange juice. The vomiting. Being bedridden for long periods of time.

"Esme…"

"Is that why he strangled me? Because he didn't want to lose me or I'm too close?"

"Yes."

"Oh. Does Bill love me or was that a lie all along?"

"I don't know. Bill can go either way as far as love goes. At least that what I got from being married to him. Because you can't kill the people you love, right?"

"Right."

The truth bitterly punched Esme right in the stomach, knocking all the air out of her. She was about to question her older sister when a noise recklessly brought her back from the land of slumber. A kind of crashing sound followed by a high-pitched shriek.

"Damn it, what now?" Esme grumbled as she dragged herself out of bed.

Fourteen

Darkness greeted Esme once she opened the bedroom door conscientiously. Braving a stretch to turn on the light on the nearest nightstand, she blinked a million times against the satiny startling brilliant fingers of fragile rays could only reached out so far. Leaving the door ajar by just a crack, she still found herself staring into the heavy darkness, vulnerable and alone.

Alone…solitary…

Yes, that's it. She felt alone. Not all her life, but right now. An unexpected stab of pain struck dead on into the very core of her heart, depleting her almost immediately. All of a sudden, she wanted to go back into her room and slam the door, protecting herself from the danger lurking somewhere in the formless dense shadows, but didn't. instead, Esme stood her ground. Her backbone ramrod straight, she was in the position of being stubborn enough to not let faintheartedness conquer her after all, though there was this little bit of terror trickling in her veins.

"I'm not afraid of you. Do you hear me?" she announced this somewhat proclamation with a brave heart and a straight face. In the pitch darkness, in one place or another, she could almost see the shadows shiver and scramble with anticipation, perhaps even a hint of cowardice. Giving rise to another notch pf courageousness inside her heavily beating heart and impatient soul, forging a fresh fire deep within her.

"Do you hear me? I'm not afraid of you!" Esme repeated with a yowl out to the vast stretch of hefty murkiness that threatened to swallow her up and spit her out in any way, shape, or form as it pleases. Add the faint cheery yellowish glow coming from her bedroom, cutting through the crack just to hold the obscurity at bay.

Nonetheless, she waited…

And waited.

For what she didn't even know or describe. She tried not to care, only to fail miserably because she was now guessing that Bill was beginning to abandon her for Amanda. Hell, as far as she was bothered and by what her gut was telling her, Bill had already dumped her for Amanda, a fact that clearly told her via what she is seeing and hearing right now.

All this darkness…

All this silence.

Again, she went back to the darkness and called out:

"Hello? Bill?"

Once again, the muteness answered her back, forcing her stomach to painfully knot itself in tight twists and turns. She is definitely *sure* that someone is here in the shadows and is certainly not Bill.

"Hello?"

Despite not feeling alone, an unsettling quietude continued to greet her coldly, formally invite her to come inside its rich dark folds. Enough for Esme to step back in fear without controlling her actions and reactions, drawing in a deep breath, calling back her bravery and strength, she didn't mind this rolling quietness and gigantic murkiness sneaking up to her in advance.

"Hello? *Oh!*"

Something strong and real swam here and there deep within the heavy seas of massive darkness, grabbed Esme by force, its hand slapped over her mouth, its snarl raw, low, and menacing:

"Shut up! Do you want to wake up your husband?"

Even though she didn't struggle, Esme stood absolutely still as her brain clanged itself around to figure out just whose voice sounds so recognizable. And then it hit her:

"Todd?"

Her captor, with a heavy sigh, could only answer her with tight squeezes and muffled grunts before rumbling in her ear:

"What are you? You and your sister…why here? Why you?"

"What do you mean, Todd?"

"Go back to bed now."

"But, Todd, you haven't answered my question—"

"Esme, bed, now!"

Todd relaxed his grip and melted back into the immense shadows, compelling Esme to sprint into her room, unwisely slamming the door shut behind her, breathing a sigh of relief while Todd's words came to haunt her as they rang themselves in her ears:

What are you? You and your sister…why here? Why you?

A knock on the door squeezed out a constrained squeak from her lips, her trembling hands clumsily work their way to turn the lock, locking the door.

"Leave me alone!"

The door clattered loud and violently in response to her terrified yelps. Clapping her hands over her ears, Esme collapsed on the bed, curling herself into a tight little ball, crying:

"Leave me alone!"

As if to taunt her, the door rattled harder, louder, and with more vehemence, making her sob and wail noisier than she has even been before. She kept on bawling and howling up until she fell fast asleep.

Fifteen

"Honey! Esme! Are you okay? Open this door!"

The knocking on and the rattling of the bedroom door and its knob was different this time, bringing about a ferocious headache right along with it. Her head pounding like everything and nothing she had ever experienced in her life, she chose to ignore the banging and hammering by simply hollering these words out to him:

"Leave me, alone, Bill!"

Bill sucked in a deep breath, exhaling in a sigh, as he softly begged, "Esme…"

"Please, Bill."

"All right. I will come back in a couple of hours, okay?"

Struggling to keep her cool, all she could do is said, "Okay."

In a heartbeat, Esme felt herself gradually relaxed in a sleeping state although her stomach grumbled and rumbled out of hunger. Rolling over into a fetal position, Esme fell fast asleep within seconds if not minutes later.

Dreaming dreamless dreams again…

"Esme."

"Mmm?"

"Esme!"

"Wha—what?"

"It's Bill. Are you hungry?"

"Yes."

"Are you going to unlock this door?"

Blowing a raspberry at the door, Esme crawled over to the bedroom door, unlocked it with a tentative twist of her wrist, and slinked back into the bed, throwing the covers over her head and body. To Bill, as he prudently opened the door only a crack, it signaled to him that his Esme really didn't want to be bothered right at this moment. With that in mind, he left her to her much-needed sleep.

She slept for a couple more hours before a hand lightly but firmly shook her awake in a certain commanding manner. Unintelligible and tetchy to a great fault, she childishly slapped away while cursing him under her breath.

"Come on, Honey. It's time to get up."

"I don't want to."

"Esme—"

"No."

"Yes."

"No!"

"Yes!"

She squawked in surprise as a strong pair of arms scooped her up against a hard chest. Wailing like a little girl, Esme wriggled for an insufficient amount of time when Bill's deep-throated voice spoke out in a very annoyed tone emphasis:

"Hey! Stop it! If you keep on thrashing around like that, I will drop your ass!"

Esme hurriedly stopped her squiggling and wiggling out of horror of being dropped on her butt by Bill who exhaled "Thank you" out of relief as he carried her with reservations right out of the bedroom and down the stairs to the dining room where he sat her in one of the chairs.

"There. You have to be hungry, right?"

Esme's stomach betrayed her by snarling loudly in response, making her blush and Bill smile.

"I take it as a 'yes'?"

Rubbing his hands enthusiastically, he chirped:

"Okay. I made some chicken noodle soup and hot tea since you are still not feeling so well."

He delicately places a piping hot bowl of soup and a hot cup of tea right in front of her. Both the soup and tea smelled so very scrumptious enough to consume, so she hungrily shoved a spoon right in, eating and drinking with ravenous delight.

"How is it?"

"Mmm…delicious. Thank you, Bill."

"You're welcome."

Bill said it with a slight smile on his lips as he watched over Esme while she feasted. Happiness swelled deep inside his heart, the realization of Esme's dependence upon him finally came into fruition. And all it took was some anti-freeze in her orange juice! Who would have thought that this highly passionate and quick irrational thinking would keep her with him!

"I'm done."

"Already? Don't you want any seconds?"

"Yes…and no. I don't want any seconds because I'm so full. Can I go to bed now?"

She frowned as she said it, her exhausted body and soul still trying to heal, to get better, on its accord. Esme hadn't heard from Joanna lately, a fact that distressed her the most because she started to wonder if she should stay or go. She knew Joanna would want her to go, but Esme is on the fence about it.

Like some devilish whirlwind, Amanda burst through the front door without any warning or greeting, beautiful and demanding as always. The blue-eyed goddess came back to taunt Esme, shoving Bill's wife into her shell out of shame and invisibility, snubbing Esme as she strode up to Bill, her eyes flashing alight with brutality, her stare icy and hurt, her voice cutting and frosty to the core as she challenged him quite dramatically:

"Have you told her?"

"Told me what, Bill?" Esme cheeped up, finding her voice after it lodge itself within the protective confines of her throat.

"Shut up, woman! Your husband is in love with *me* and *I* love him and we're going to get out of this town *together* once you're taken care of."

"Oh…"

"Amanda! Damn it!" Bill roared, slamming down his fists on the table so hard that it startled Esme and upset the dishes in turn, their clattering and clinking in protest and reaction to Bill's feedback to Amanda and her poorly timed announcement.

"But Bill," Amanda whined and pouted, obviously hurt by his angry brash demeanor and conduct in the direction of her.

"What does she mean?" Esme's voice held a strong yet dangerous note of wounded and fury. Her sparkling topaz eyes glittered and watered with hot pricking tears threatening to fall as everything crumbled all around her. For once in her life, Esme's heartbreak has grown to force her at long last.

For Bill, however, this drama couldn't have happened at such an inopportune time because it now looked like his wife is currently facing the actual thought of leaving him for good. Roughly seizing Amanda by the left forearm, hauling her kicking and screaming to the front door.

"Ow! Face it, Bill…I'm better and prettier than your plain Jane Esme! You and I belong together!"

With an inconsolable cry, Esme scampered up to her room, banging the door shut with a reverberation of its lock at the same time as Amanda yelped and howled with unruly laughter. Cursing up a blue streak and visibly maddened with this damned spectacle, Bill callously shoved Amanda out of the door, roughly dragged her back to her own house.

Comfortably locked in her own room, Esme flung herself on the bed, curling her spastic body into a tight fetal position as she cried her eyes out up until she hiccupped and fell fast asleep. Once more, she was dreaming of dreamless dreams and forgotten shadows.

Sixteen

Once again, Esme dozed for so long that she could have slept forever and ever if she wanted to. Still curled up in a little human ball, she wondered why she felt all twisted and cramped until she evoked each and every one of those happenings that occurred last night, triggering her to bawl her eyes out all over again. Huge tears of sorrow and pain seeping and hiding deep inside her broken heart for years. All it needed was a trigger to bust that dam.

And, boy, did the dam break…

Realizing she didn't have sufficient strength to stop the tears anymore, all the anguish and mourning Esme endured during her life and marriage still burns her soul right into the ground.

"Damn Bill and damn Amanda too!" she seethed into the pillow, sobbing hysterically as she let the tears flow. "I am so done with him!"

"Good girl!"

"Joanna?"

A cool breeze faintly skulked in, gently brushing Esme's left cheek like a sisterly kiss despite Joanna being a ghost. Thanks in part to her sister being here, Esme truly experienced she belonged even though her own marriage is falling apart.

"I'm glad you're back, Joanna."

"I'm happy to be back."

"Where were you?" Esme inquired, slightly embarrassed to sound like a spoiled child. Nevertheless, Joanna didn't mind for she responded sincerely:

"I was kind of banished by Bill for a little while. The herbs he used were not so strong as he thought. I think he used the herbs and spell properly."

"He didn't do his spell right or used old herbs?"

"Both."

"Why did you come back?"

"Because you still need help, Esme. You need to get out of this house."

"Oh, yes, I know that now."

"What happened?"

"One word: Amanda."

"Oh."

"Yes, Joanna…oh…"

Esme began to cry again, her tears and sobs more watery and harder than ever before. Coiling herself in a ball as a protection from the harsh world, she grasped it didn't stop the heartbreak.

"I think we better start to get away start to get ready to get away from Bill" Joanna softly suggested while Esme hemmed and swayed in her own grief and loss.

"I think so, too, but how?"

"I think Bill isn't home right now. If he isn't, I believe we should take advantage of this."

"Okay."

With a heavy heart and heavier limbs, Esme lugged the two suitcases she brought her, plopping them on the bed. With a stubborn determination, she took her dear sweet time un taking her clothes and things out of the closet and drawers, delicately folding them and placing them in the suitcases each in its appropriate spot. Just as long as the door is locked, Esme is so very bound and resolve to let go of Bill and his dangerous ways.

There, she mentioned inside her head, finalizing everything between Bill and her mentally.

"Esme…Esme!"

Shit…

Bill's voice slipped through the door while his hands shook and rattled the door knob. Knocking from time to time, he kept on calling her name until she couldn't take it anymore.

"Bill, go back to Amanda! She needs you more than me!"

Silence followed in its own quaint way and then:

"Amanda is gone."

She stopped packing, her heart stuttering to a halt as her brain devours the words with great care. Amanda's gone? How?

"Gone. What do you mean, gone?"

"She left me when I told her that all I want is you and us."

"Oh Bill. You should have stopped Amanda and went with her. I don't want you and us. Just leave me alone in peace so I can get out of here."

Silence followed once more, then, all of a sudden, the burdensome crashing of a body slamming against the door over and over again, wrenching high-pitched screams from Esme, making this too melodramatic even for someone like her.

"No, Esme! I won't leave you leave me! You can't leave me! You won't!"

"Leave me alone!" she wailed piercingly, violently slapping her hands against the door over and over until her palms were red and stinging. "Go back to Amanda! She wants you and she's better and prettier than me!"

"I tell you Amanda doesn't want me anymore."

"Liar!"

"Esme, please believe me…"

"No!"

"Esme, Honey…"

"Bill, if you really love me, please leave me alone and go back to your Amanda," Esme bawled, not caring how childish she sounded along the way; her body, mind, heart, and soul already tenderized, shattered, and hollowed out of any emotions past the point of no return.

"You must be strong, little sister. Don't let Bill get inside your head," Joanna rang in, her voice giving away a stern warning.

"Shut up, Joanna! It's too late. Bill is already inside my head," Esme blubbered out, her tears cascading down her cheeks like twin waterfalls.

Once again, the stillness arose from the other side of the door where Bill stood, his words low, raw, and broken:

"Is Joanna in there?"

"Yes."

"Get rid of her *now*."

"No."

"Esme—"

"*No!* I will not get rid of my sister just because you want me to."

"Okay…okay…I will leave you alone. For now."

"Thank you."

An easy-going hush energetically developed into a fixed fixture on the side where Bill used to stand. Over on her side, Esme definitively detected a kind of improved reprieve and hope granted as she finished packing up and shutting each suitcase with a reassuring click.

"There."

"Good. Now let's go," Joanna gasped, happy to see Esme certainly took the first step towards quitting Bill and his poisonous ways forever.

Throwing herself into the engrossed darkness that welcomed and scared Esme when she opened the door, she felt her stomach heaved and go all topsy turvy on her at the first sight of this heavy murkiness. All the wild excitement and stomach-churning fear, forced her to straightened up her shoulders, steal a shaky breath, and unhurriedly crept into this enormous obscurity which swallowed her whole right along with her two suitcases.

With great care, she twists and turn her path around the furniture, all bathed in the dark, clumsily colliding with pieces here and there, cussing under her breath even as she struggled to keep her tight hold on her two weighty suitcases, until she got to the front door.

Taking in a deep breath, she was about to cautiously open the door when a shadowy hand reeking of a sickly-sweet hospital disinfectant clamped tight and hard over her nose and mouth, compelling her to scream out a weakly protest as the fumes invade her nose and mouth productively. Suffering a wild dizzying spell as well as a case of substantial lethargy, Esme freefall into a vast unconscious state where the dreamless dreams drift through the inside of her fuzzy brain like a ship sailing through a fog-laden ocean.

"Esme! Esme! Where are you?" Joanna's anxious calls echoed and pinged into the faraway nothingness.

I'm over here! Here! Esme wished for her voice to come out of her and into a loud yell, but no sound took place, much to Esme's disappointment as she floated away into the foreign hills, valleys, and rivers of the unknown.

Seventeen

“Ugh...my head...”

Esme woke up bone-weary, weak-kneed, and with a raging pounding headache that knew no end. Undergoing an icky moment in which she wasn't too sure if she was about to throw up or not, she warily flipped onto her left side without any plans to sit up anytime soon. One more time, her headache throbbed irritably at her for executing such a stupid move in its opinion, driving her to groan and whimper all at the same time.

“Ugh...”

She bleated once more with this time weeping hot burning tears, her headache turning into a difficult little beast to her. Not too impressed with her head exploding into a million stars, Esme took some very deep breaths even as she noiselessly mulled over any possible notions while lounging in a bed, eyes closed, lost between being wide awake and slumberland.

Wait...

Why am I in bed?

Nonchalantly opening her eyes, Esme realized the same familiar positions of the bedroom without spending time remembering it all. After all, she literally *knew* this bedroom for approximately a week or so.

Oh crap...

“Bill! Damn him...*ow!*”

Delicately sitting up in her bed, her intensified headache ebbing and flowing, Esme peered all around her and ended up suffering somewhat disillusionment. She was back in the master bedroom *and* in the house!

Meaning she had never left….

Oh, how she would love to scream out in fear, fury, and frustration had it not been for this stupid headache!

"Ugh…"

Slowly turning herself away from the door, Esme plopped herself down on its familiar softness and fell into a lackluster sleep out of sheer boredom and disappointment since she easily assumed there is nothing for her to do.

"Ugh!"

Repeating this one word with reaction one more time, once more with feeling born from a coughing mixture of tediousness and vexation combined. Yawning for a single moment, Esme flopped over to her right side and fell fast asleep.

Minutes passed then hours before a cool breeze sneaked itself inside her bedroom.

"Esme."

"Joanna."

"Esme!"

Joanna roughly shook her younger sister's right shoulder in a hard desperate attempt to wake Esme up. Nervous erratic shakes of her shoulder were enough for Esme to firmly say:

"Leave me alone, Joanna! Can't you see that I am trapped in here with no place to go?"

"Esme!"

Hearing the hurt in Joanna's voice, Esme suddenly felt sad and sorry that she begged her older sister:

"Please don't be mad at me, Joanna. Please."

"I'm not mad at you, little sister, just scared for you, that's all."

"I care about you too, Joanna. Thank you for being here."

"Aww…that is so sweet! If a ghost like me could cry real tears, I would."

"Oh, Joanna, please don't cry or else I will cry too."

"Don't cry and don't worry, Esme. I will find a way to get you out of here safely."

"So, what do you want me to do?"

"Rest."

"Rest?"

"That's all you can do, little sister."

"Oh."

On the other side of the door, Bill didn't sleep as much or as easier as he would like to, such as he has done with the others. Just like Esme, his dreams were dreamless but unlike Esme, Joanna kept on hiding in the shadows of his dreams. Simmering shadows that covers Joanna so very well if only for a little while.

"Why don't you let Esme go? You have Amanda and Amanda has you."

"Because Esme is *all mine*! You hear me? *Mine!* Not *yours*!

"That's where you are wrong, Bill, because Esme is my family. My sister. Blood is thicker than water right here, right now."

"I'm not wrong! You're wrong!"

A harsh chuckle rose out of nowhere and somewhere in the vast darkness. Deep and almost evil sounding, it told him, hell, even <u>reminded</u> him about the demon living inside his head whenever he pops off the deep end of his mind. Right now, his mind is crystal clear and calculating—a dangerous combination to be sure. At least, for Esme's sake because that's when he becomes desperate.

"How am I wrong, Bill?", Joanna taunted.

"Amanda is not mine and I am not hers. *Esme* is mine and I am *hers*."

"Bull."

"What did you say?"

"I said 'Bull', Bill."

Had it been a different time and place, Bill would have found his conversation absurdly funny to his egotistical soul is stuck with Joanna and her crazy soul.

Speaking of Joanna…

"It's time for you to wake up, Bill. Right…about…now."

Bill woke up with a frightful start, complete panic rummaging through his tense veins and arteries as he rushed up the stairs to Esme's door, his fingers fumbling with the keys while his left hand tested the knob to see if it is locked like he locked it. Satisfied with the door being locked, he shoved the keys back into his right pocket and stomped back down the stairs to the couch. Laying down on the couch, he felt peace settle over him as he fell fast asleep to dreamless dreams without Joanna hanging around in them.

Eighteen

sme snoozed so fitfully and deeply that she didn't notice the slow crawling change from day to night nor didn't even hear the lock boldly click to open and Bill stealing the chance to sneak in. She didn't even detected the full moon creeping in through the windows, making him relaxed to the point he didn't see the make figure concealed ever so delicately in the shadows, watching over Esme like a protective silent hawk.

Todd experienced some restlessness and a readiness to fight once his eyes caught the moonlit spectacle of Bill arriving in the room, taking privilege in sitting on her bed so very close to her, staring at her doze free from any chance of disturbing her. Positively sure he didn't interrupt Esme and her peaceful sleep, Bill simply sat there, suffering both excitement and nervous at the same time while Todd, her unassigned protector, bore edginess and protection and God knows what else, tense and taut like a bow, ready to draw an arrow to strike at his boss at any given time, damned the consequences.

Deep in his madly beating heart, Bill comprehended he loved her with a possessive vengeance and would do anything to keep her away from everyone, including Todd, Amanda, and especially Joanna. Stroking his wife's hair, Bill sensed this gist of accepting on Esme's part and anticipated on her receiving him and his love for her once again, to trust him again, to forget about what he did to her as well as Amanda and her hurtful words forever.

"Shit", Bill groused, knowing he had to take care of Amanda before taking care of Esme.

Simple…so damned simple…

Sucking in a yawning breath, Bill rose from the bed, his face hidden from the moon and stoic with thoughts. Thoughts about Esme and their fragile sickly marriage. Thoughts about Amanda and their passion-filled but highly destructive relationship. Thoughts about Joanna and their failed dead marriage and its tormented ghost of an afterlife.

"Damn it!"

He was aware of his need to call or call on Amanda. To get things in order or just simply finish things, Bill no longer knew or cared as long as Amanda was put to rights, so to speak. Deciding to call her, he disregarded his sleeping wife only to settle on Amanda without making a decisive choice in the matter. Fetching the cell phone out of his right back pants pocket, Bill's steady finger quickly picked off Amanda's number for what he hopes to be one last time.

"Hello, Bill."

Amanda's voice betrayed her excitement by adding a little breathy squeal of joy at the sound of his breathing, patiently waiting for him to talk to her.

"Hey, Amanda. What's up?" he squirmed as his voice sounded dull and fake. Just like the question he asked her.

"I'm fine. What's up?"

"We need to talk."

"In person or over the phone?"

"In person."

"Oh…okay," her gasping sounded more like a balloon losing air instead of being used as a sensual seduction instrument.

"I will be there in a couple of minutes."

Bill made sure to smoothly sneak out of the bedroom as noiselessly as possible, locking it up real tight before stealing down the stairs and out of the house.

As soon as Todd was certain Bill is out of the house and headed for the house he shared with Amanda, thank God for windows, he snuck right up to the bed where Esme is sleeping in like a thief in the night. Stealing a spot where his boss sat, he sat perfectly still without bothering her and her sleep. Stealing a glance, Todd found himself dazzled by the moonlight shimmering and washing all over his boss' wife as if she was a mermaid sleeping under water in the ocean. Peaceful and beautiful, Todd came to a decision devoid of any prejudice.

"You deserve better, Miss Esme."

Todd whispered those words more to himself rather than to her, his hands itching something fierce to touch and stroke her hair, black and shiny as a raven's wing, in a gentle caress. She looked so much like Joanna that his heart ached in a lover's painful sense of yearning.

Why did Bill pick Esme? What is he repeating? Todd's mind wondered at a worrying state. *Why these twin sisters? What is Bill up to with them?*

Strutting along the garden trail towards Amanda's little cottage located some twenty feet or so from the main house, Bill grew both enthusiastic and impatient all at the same time, taking in several deep breaths in order to calm himself down as he wandered onto that old acquainted trail.

Reaching Amanda's front door, Bill's knuckles rapped softly on the green-painted door, ready and waiting only a few seconds until Amanda flew open the door, her voice a high-pitched squeak that nearly busted his eardrums.

"Bill!"

"Hello, Amanda."

"Come in, come in. You sound so…formal."

"Well, you know, we have to keep up with appearances until Esme is gone."

"That's right! I totally forgot about that! So, when is that going to happen?"

"Whenever I am ready to have her gone or she runs out of her usefulness, which is very soon. One way or another, Amanda."

"Are you serious? About us, I mean."

"What a silly question. Yes, I am sincere about us, Amanda."

"Sincere…that's another word for serious, right?"

"Of course."

"Well?"

"Well, what?"

"Stop kidding and be real," Amanda whined crossly as she hit him on the right shoulder. "Answer my question."

"What is the question?"

"I don't know. I forgot, "she wailed, her pitch squeaky and ear-piercing before lowering her tone back to normal.

With Amanda's back to him, she didn't comprehended Bill slipping on a pair of latex gloves without a sound, his icy blue stare fully trained on Amanda's back. His gloved hands longing to grab her neck and throttle her, Bill calmly but soundlessly lurked up to her. Wrapped up in a combination of thrill and determination, he dared himself to reach out and gently but firmly massage her neck and back in circular strokes.

"Mmm…that feels so good. Why don't you do this with me before?" Amanda purred as he kneaded her back up to her neck, back to her back, and back to her neck once again, lingering around her neck a little longer than usual. Stealing this moment to take advantage, Bill's gloved fingers crawled around her neck and squeezed tighter and tighter with each second.

"Hey! What are you doing?" Amanda croaked, her fingers clawing and digging into his fingers and her neck as she struggled to breathe and for freedom. "Stop!"

Turning a blind eye to her headstrong will, her hoarse screams, and fight to live, he kept on constricting his grasp, telling her in a reassuring tone:

"Shh…it's okay…"

Her eyes widened in terror, Amanda trued her dogged best to pry his super strong fingers from her neck in a fierce battle for air, still fighting for her own life until the moment came when she just can't combat for her life anymore.

"Stop fighting it, Amanda. It will be so very easy to simply let it happen…ow! You bitch!" an annoyed Bill growled into her left ear as finally got the chance to scratch his fresh wound on his right hand and wrist and forearm, forcing his hands to squeezed even stronger.

Amanda gurgled and gasped while in the throes of struggling and fighting between life and death, against the pain and darkness now threatening to swallow her whole in a heartbeat. She knew somehow, she was losing this game and, boy, is she failing quickly!

"Just let go, Amanda."

Bill hummed in her left ear, almost as if he was either hypnotizing her or pleading with her. All of a sudden, she given up the ghost, her struggles worn down into nothingness, fatigue washing over her at last even as she died slowly and surely. Enjoying the pleasure of observing the life steadily ebb away from her eyes, Bill simply left her lying on the kitchen floor after dragging her from the living room and into the kitchen. Locking the front door behind him, he looked both ways and all around him as he walked back to his house, stripping off his gloves and tossing them in the outdoor trash can, thankful that nobody noticed him doing so.

Or was he?

Shuffling through the murkiness, watching Bill dump his gloves in the trash can, stood a shadow that seemed to shimmer within the darkness before being swallowed whole by the shadows.

Stalking up to the front door, key in hand, Bill didn't seem to be in a hurry as he unlocked the door and quietly entered the house without incident. Silence welcomed him home, causing him to worry immediately.

Is Esme still here?

Worry grew into dread; he wandered up the stairs towards the bedroom door. Unlocking the door and turning the knob slowly, Bill breathed a sigh of relief when he saw Esme all by herself, sleeping soundly in her bed.

"Thank you."

He whispered his gratitude to her and yet no one in particular. Turning away from the bed, he kept the door unlocked, rewarding her for staying.

Now to address the ghost in the room:

"Let's face it, Joanna. I won. You lost. Esme tried to escape from me, but failed. Get over it," Bill challenged to nowhere and everywhere. Through clenched teeth, he proudly proclaimed his victory even as he went downstairs to the couch for some rest after a long day.

"Esme! Esme!"

"Shh—Joanna."

"What should we do?"

"I don't know, Joanna, I just don't know."

Esme pondered over what she should do, her heart pounding a mile a minute and her head swimming through a thick fogged ocean, her wide topaz eyes trained themselves directly on the door, waiting with tempted breath up until she finally fell back into a tuckered-out sleep.

Nineteen

The dreamless dreams appeared in her head once again, constructing Esme to catch some forty winks relaxingly as a log. Even the slight chill of the ghostly Joanna roaming around didn't stir Esme from her deep sleep.

"Esme! Esme!"

"Wha—what?" Esme snorted, flopping and thrashing like a fish caught in a net. "Joanna! What do you want?"

"We have to go."

"Now?"

"Yes, Esme, now."

"Joanna, we tried it before and look what happened! I got drugged and locked up in this room!"

"But little sister…no! no, Esme! Don't fall asleep!"

"Okay…okay! I'm awake, okay?"

"No, it's not okay. It's time to go!"

Wrangling to get up, Esme carped and whined her way to the closet. Opening the closet door wide…

No suitcases.

"Hey, where are my—Bill! Bill stole my suitcases!" Esme fumed, perfectly dismayed with Bill's meddling in her life and life decisions.

"Oh no!" Joanna cried, angry that Bill pinched Esme's luggage on purpose, his clear intention being able to trap Esme in this house forever. Joanna fuming that he dared to pilfer Esme's two suitcases, the only things she ever owned, she would have gladly punched a wall on her sister's behalf if she wasn't a ghost.

"Now what can I do, Joanna?" Esme's voice cracked with raw pained emotion, pushing Joanna to direct her attention back to her younger sister.

"We—you have to leave with the clothes on your back."

Nodding dumbly in agreement, Esme mentally readied herself to leave both this house and her husband with nothing but the clothes she is wearing right now. Sucking in a deep breath to herself and her nerves, she crept soundlessly over to the bedroom door. Testing the doorknob, she was surprised to find it not resisting to her twists. Opening the door with a soft click, she stared into the endless gloom. Glancing left then right, her eyes strained to look fixedly into the dimness. Here in the obscurity, Esme glued her eyes upon the things stirring beneath the shadows. Dread took possession of her ferociously beating heart, leading Esme to struggle to keep her breath slow and even. Washed down in the darkness, she discreetly took straggling baby steps that seemed like forever.

So far, so good...

Still maintaining her breath relaxed and smooth, Esme vigilantly touched and advanced her way close to the front door. She was doing so damned good before the coming of a two-timing squeak from the floorboards.

Shit...

Drawing in her breath, her heart rattling to the point she could have sworn it was going to burst right out of her chest. Over there, up here, somewhere, Bill was fast asleep—or so she truly thought and hoped. Over here, the front door was beckoning her to come, uncomplainingly anticipating her to come. All she had to do was to get there. A shuffling noise over her left shoulder caught her completely unaware, freezing her to where she stood right then and there. Taking in another deep breath, she listened in vain for any more movement, any sign of Bill waking up. After a couple of minutes, Esme heard nothing much to her relief.

Almost there...

Another screechy squeak and another effort at sucking in her breath in response.

Bound and determined as ever, Esme kept right on creeping along towards the front door. Attempting to be brave, waiting for any reaction coming from Bill.

At first, she felt guilty about leaving her husband before the dissatisfied angry feeling about him snuck back inside both her head and heart.

Locked!

"Damn!" she muttered under her breath as she turned the doorknob right and left, trying her best to haltingly open the door only to find it resisting against her. Groaning, she gave up quickly and slinked back to her room, defeated and lost.

"Esme? Are you here, Honey?"

Oh shit…

Suddenly thankful for the darkness to conceal her true facial and body reactions, Esme gulped down her fear and simply said," Yes, I was about to go to the kitchen for a glass of water."

"In the dark?"

"Yes. Why not?"

"Oh…it's nothing."

It was only one little sentence, but it was enough to make Esme breathe a sigh of relief. Noiselessly strolling back to her room, she was almost there when she heard Bill's sleepy voice whispering up to her from downstairs:

"Are you going to bed now?"

"Yes."

"What about your water?"

Esme stood very still, undecided at how to answer him at all. Nevertheless, she straightened her backbone, responding the best way she could:

"Oh, well, it can wait."

"Okay. Good night."

"Good night."

Closing the door behind her with a loud click, Esme felt trapped and alone until she remembered the windows. Cautiously sneaking towards the windows, she lightly pulled open the curtains and discovered the window have been nailed shut! Whimpering inwardly, she went to the other window just as quietly as she possibly can.

The same!

What? How?

What and how, indeed. She didn't recall hearing the deafening pounding of a hammer's head striking the nails. Or the muted strain of her husband's working on the windows.

When did this happened?

Again, Esme took to wracking her brain, trying to make sense of it all. Did he do this when she was sick? He must have done it using her illness to his advantage.

Looking back, Esme simply recalled the sickly sugared taste in her orange juice, by all means, orange juice and oranges can be sweet, *but not that sugary sweet*! Of course, it didn't help that Bill poured something that made her sick without a hitch.

"Bill…that bastard…"

Anger silently simmered and released itself from the very intimate care of her heart and soul, sucking in all of his betrayal in order to keep her with him.

"Damn him!"

Esme howled these two words at the windows, her fury boiling up till it met with its threat to kick up a row if she grants it. A slow burn she never knew existed until now.

"I *will* get out of here and never see him again," she seethed. "I *will* leave him. *That's* for sure."

"*Good girl*," whispered Joanna, proud that Esme has finally see the light. "What are you going to do now?"

"Go to bed."

Twenty

Esme snoozed previously to hearing the high-pitched droning whine of sirens coming from the outside. In the character of snooping or perhaps some other form of curiosity, she took a chance to open her bedroom door just a tad bit wider than she expected and climbed down the stairs in a cautious manner towards the front door. When she got there, she found the door padlocked, much to her dismay.

"Argh!"

Slinking around and around the house, she abruptly thought about the upstairs windows again. Clambering up the stairs once more, she opened the door with the full intent of inspecting the second bedroom windows. Wandering into the second bedroom, Esme found the room still empty but the windows seemed to be free from any nail that threatened to fastened it.

"Yay."

Happiness danced wildly in his heart, hope danced in her soul, Esme used all her strength to throw up the window sash wide open, wide enough so she can fit through. Another surge of hopefulness moved her in the strange direction of slipping through the open window, landing quite awkwardly in fully grown rose bushes.

"Ow…ow…ouch!"

With each and every move, the deep-seated cuts drove themselves all across her face, arms, legs, and body, drawing a good amount of blood here and there, perhaps a little bit more than the other grazes, depending on how she landed. Stinging lacerations, torn clothing, and tenderized gashes, she could almost swear that the bruises will soon show themselves. Rolling inelegantly off the rose bushes and into a strong pair of comforting arms, Esme was helped into standing. Limping a little, she tried to act somewhat normal despite the pain, the mess she seems like as she walk-limp her way from the house.

"Esme—um—Missus Porcher, where are you going?"

"Away from here. From him."

"Good."

"Good?"

She burst out laughing as she kept right on walk-limping. Whatever action happened was no longer around. She was really all alone, making her more vulnerable than she anticipated.

No wait…

"Todd?"

"Yes, Esme?"

"Ahh!"

"Esme!"

As she fell face forward, a strong pair of arms came back to grab her and hold her tight against a sturdy protective chest, providing her with all the warmth and support she ever needed and more.

"Ow…crap…"

Hunched over in pain, her arms crossed to cover some of the scratches that decorated her arms in a crisscross and ragged straight-lined fashion, she wanted so much to scurry away down the dirt path, away from the house as fast as she could feasibly can had it not been for Todd and his amazing arms of strength and glory holding her still and close to him. Head down, Esme tried to force her legs to straightened themselves up and her feet to flattened themselves onto the ground in a standing, albeit staggering, position. Trying to steady and ready herself to break into a run, not caring where she was just as long as she was far away from Bill.

"Are you okay?"

"Yes…Todd…no…"

Esme gasped as an unexpected darkness swirled and danced around her before swallowing her whole in a state of unconsciousness.

"Esme!"

Todd was quick to snatch Esme up and away into his arms without a struggle. Holding her close to him, he chose to take Mister Porcher's wife to his small cabin on the property, damning the aftermaths.

Almost there…

"Todd? Todd! What are you doing here and what are you doing with my wife?"

In Todd's ears, he thought he heard shock in Mister Porcher's tone, telling him what he already guessed when he found his sister's lifeless body lying on the kitchen floor. The police speculated about him as they kept on asking him the questions that they considered hard-nosed enough, hoping to trip him up.

Certain questions like:

"Where were you when your sister was killed?"

"In town."

"Doing what?"

"Buying parts for the sink."

"Do you have proof?"

"If you mean receipts, yes, I do."

"Well, don't leave town. We might have more questions."

"The door is always opened, officer."

And now he had somewhat lackluster proof that Mister Porcher killed his sister. In fact, he was absolutely *certain* his sister's boss did the deed.

"Hello, Mister Porcher."

Todd took a moment to spot Esme wincing in his arms even though he reckoned it was just a reply to Bill as the other man come up to Todd tower over Esme and him regardless of the fact that Todd is a few inches taller than the other man.

"You haven't answered my questions."

Quick thinking as usual, Todd kept his voice calm and easy:

"Well, I still live here even though my sister is dead. As to Missus Porcher, she is hurt. I was going to take her to my cabin and fix her up."

"Why?"

"Why not?"

Esme stirred in his arms, eyes opening just a crack, as she snuggled against him, her voice low and weak:

"Don't give me to him. Please save me. He's trying to kill me. Please."

She grimaced once more, this time at how flat and feeble she appeared to her ears. How her heart leaped in fear and anxiety. She strained to straightened her backbone only to have Todd shift her body into a more comfortable position for himself.

"Ma'am?"

Woozy but still wise enough to play dumb, Esme raised her tone of voice, hoping Todd is smart enough to take the hint:

"Todd? I thought you were Bill."

Seizing the implication, he cleverly nodded ever so slightly before apologizing to Esme in a calm yet gentle way:

"I'm so sorry for confusing you, Ma'am."

"That's okay. Thank you for saving me, Todd."

"You're welcome, Missus Porcher."

"Where were you going, Esme?" Bill demanded, his arms reaching out to grab his wife in an automatic reaction. She cringed involuntarily and noticeably as Todd reluctantly passed her over to Bill's outstretched arms.

"Now, Esme, are you going to tell exactly where were you moving on to?" he hammered ever so lightly and demandingly.

Taking a deep mouthful of air, she dares herself to lie ever so sweetly and defiantly, hoping against hope that Todd would notice this tiny falsehood.

"Oh, I just went out for a walk."

"That's it?"

"Yep."

However, if Todd or Bill detected her lie, both men didn't let her know as Bill went on with his questioning:

"You look terrible, Honey. Have you fallen into something?"

"The rose bush."

"Ouch."

"So, I guess it's time for you to go home and get fixed up there," Todd murmured wretchedly to Esme, noting the spark of horror snapping in her beautiful topaz eyes, but too helpless to do anything.

But it was Esme who betrayed her true feelings, her voice rising into a full-hearted screech, her arms stretched out in a need of assistance.

"Oh no! No! please! Don't let me go back to Bill!" she cried out, capturing Bill's attention as a result.

Stuck in between a rock and a hard place, Todd had to call out, his voice strained with worry and anxiety as he gently coax, kind and considerate to her plight while his mind running a hundred million miles a minute.

"Oh, come now, Missus Porcher, your husband needs you."

But in Esme's mind the tone in Todd's voice communicated to her that he meant to take her back to Bill without any protest or trouble from her. That he meant business as well as his interest in keeping his cabin, Todd was bound and determined to take her back, even by force, to the house.

Her prison…

Peeking over her husband's shoulder, Esme saw the hurt look crossing Todd's eyes as he mouthed her name:

Esme.

Save me, Todd, please, she mimed back.

I…can't. I'm sorry. As much as I want to, he's the one in charge.

Nodding in dejected understanding, Esme had no choice except to cling frantically to her husband. Feeling dizzy when Bill twirled around to face Todd, his voice declaring himself satisfied and happy with the other man for finding his wife.

"Thank you, Todd, for bringing my wife back to me. Otherwise, I wouldn't have known that she is an adventurous type."

"Be careful, Mister Porcher. Your adventuresome wife is awfully hurt."

"Don't worry, Todd. I will take real good care of her."

"Bill, I—"

"Shut up and don't say a damn word," Bill snarled deep into her left ear, his arms constricting themselves into a bruising squeeze against the open wounds and fresh bruises scattered all over her body, initiating a yelp from her out of pain as she watched Todd walk away.

Plopping her down hard on her feet in front of the front door, Bill twisted the knob and swung it open for her before he callously shoves her inside. Tumbling to the floor, Esme felt that Bill wanted her to see him lock and padlock the front door to confirm her prison-like state of affairs inside this house. Pocketing the keys for extra dramatic knack, he calmly turned around to face her, his icy blue eyes cold and lifeless as a dead person's.

For her part, Esme suffered from a case of being frightened and all alone. Last time, she was brave enough to plan her escape, her husband poisoned her. Even now she doesn't know what to think in regards to her punishment. Probably another atrocious way, she easily assumed.

"Bill—"

"Shut up, you stupid bitch!" Bill shouted, his fist closed up to knock her around, striking her in the face and body until her lips split and spurted blood, additional bruises forming on her cheeks, legs, and arms, forcing her to screech out in agony and suffering, her soul breaking and shattering into a million of fragments with each blow, leaving her stunned and near death as far as she was concerned.

"Go to your room or I will show you a fate worse than death. I won't ask you again," Bill cautioned her, his icy stare glittering and snapping with to some degree dangerous, something she has never seen in her short-lived marriage to him.

Terrified, she did as she was told without being so stupid as to stop and ask why, she crawled on her hands and knees as fast as she could possibly can, ignoring the smashed tender parts of her knees and hands yelling out to her in immense pain. Slithering inside and slamming the door behind her, she collapsed right in front of the door from the immeasurable amounts of pain creeping around her bowed down body, too wounded to slink over to crumple on the bed. She was too injured to even noticed the lock clicking to keep her as a prisoner of this room much less have the strength to cry her eyes and heart out.

"Oh, Esme, I'm so very sorry. I thought Todd would help you," Joanna muttered in a comforting tone, softly stroking her younger sister's hair with icy fingers. "I had hoped that would escape Bill by now."

Esme began to cry involuntarily, her voice shaking, "Me too. What do I do now?"

"I don't know. I really don't know."

Esme sobbed once again until she had fell asleep at last.

"I will try to find a way to get you out of here safe and sound," Joanna vowed to her little sister just before she vanished into thin air.

Twenty-One

With all the bawling she did in the trapped confines of her bedroom, Esme woke up with an amazing headache and her body stiff and sore. Not a simple diminutive pain behind the eyes, oh no, but a full-blown hammer-like blows knocking all around deep inside her head. The kind of strikes that kept getting stronger with each and every move she made in regards to her head. Her head still on the pillows, Esme flinched in great suffering, tears forming and falling from her tired and achy eyes.

"Ow...ow...ow..."

"Ow" was all Esme could mumble as her limbs felt too heavy and too tender with every attempted move. Nevertheless, the next thing she muttered was the name of the only person she could rely on:

"Joanna."

Like a faint flash of sunny white light, Joanna appeared to Esme similar to an angel of vengeance, undoubtedly noticing her younger sister lying in a sluggish state of pain, bruises, and cuts, infuriating the older sister more than she could ever be enraged while worrying her hook, line, and sinker.

"Esme!"

"Oh, Joanna, I'm so tired...my head and body...hurts a lot."

Esme mewled pathetically, coughing a little bit here and there, scowling in some kind of knee-jerk reaction to whatever was torturing her either physically or imaginary right on the spot...

"Help...me..."

Tied up in knots, Joanna hastily floated herself into the kitchen, suspicious about Esme's lethargy. Finding the gas stove on without a flame, her ghostly ears caught the faint hissing of the gas releasing itself into the closed off air.

Completely horrified, Joanna mustered up adequate energy to turn off the stove as safely as she possibly can. With that done, Esme's older sister forced herself to rest for a tiny bit before gathering up enough energy to unlock and drag the back door open. It took another couple of minutes to rest before gaining plenty of focusing power to open up all the windows and the front door to let the fresh air in. Sitting on a kitchen chair by the small kitchen table, spitting nails as she fumes:

"That bastard!"

Joanna snarled through her ghostly teeth, her glowing wraithy eyes seized the sight of tiny holes scattered all over the kitchen windows and a couple of holes on the door and the door jamb. So, Bill had not only nailed the windows shut he made sure that all the windows are fastened shut and the doors padlocked to make it look like Esme freaked out about something coming in and accidentally committed suicide. With a great rumbling of anger and frustration, Joanna flew up to Esme's bedroom and used all her energy to throw up the window sashes without any hesitation. That being done, Joanna spun around to take care of her younger sister.

"Come on, little sister, breathe. Please breathe. Please," Joanna softly begged, noticing the bright pinkness of Esme's skin, hoping against hope that she arrived in the nick of time. She was about to give up hope when Esme hacked and wheezed in involuntary impulse to the cool fresh air and Joanna's pleading, making Joanna pleased and her ghostly heart light.

"Esme…"

"Joanna…"

"I'm here."

"What happened?" Esme uttered huskily, still struggling to catch her breath and stay awake.

"Bill tried to kill you by using gas from the kitchen stove. Apparently, he wanted it to look like you committed suicide."

"Even when he beat me up so badly?"

"Yep."

"Is that why the doors and windows were nailed and pad-locked shut?"

"Yep, again."

"That bastard!"

"My thoughts exactly."

"So, what do we do?"

"Try to give Bill enough rope to hang himself with because he can't keep on doing this."

"I totally agree."

A soft cool breeze tenderly stroked Esme's flaming red and purplish-blue left cheek, bringing it back to its somewhat normal color, causing Joanna delighted to see Esme safe and sound even if she is still trapped inside this house.

"How are you feeling, little sister?"

"Better and worse because he certainly beat the crap out of me when we got in this house."

Esme shuddered at the memory of her husband's hands formed into livid fists landing hard blows all over her face and body like she was a punching bag,

"Once you get out of this house, you can recover properly although I am not sure how you can mend mentally."

"Should I get out now?"

"While I should think that you should…no, you especially need to save all your strength. Then, that way, we can figure out at hoe to get you out of here safely." Joanna replied, her voice sounded worn and tired out with worry. She aimed to be positive about the while thing as she watched Esme fall back asleep, her coloring better and her breathing healthier. Being a realist, even in death, Joanna was visibly afraid for Esme and wish that she is strong enough to succeed in surviving Bill and his sick and twisted ways. And just as much as Joanna was plainly troubled for her younger sister's problems and any of the possible outcomes coming Esme's way, she must protect Esme no matter what.

"Just rest. Let me try to figure out how to get you out of this place safely."

Twenty-Two

At last, Esme had her dream. More like a nightmare, it came into a tighter focus while she still dreamt of the heavy darkness sprayed and sprinkled with slotted rays of intense light. Scampering into the safety of the well-lit mist, Esme ventured to stay away from the fuzzy murkiness only to be scratched and cut by hands studded with razor-sharp fingernails cut and honed into knife-pointed points. Their scores drew blood even as she thrashed to be free up until a wooden stake rapidly came from out of nowhere, poking here, there, and everywhere from the shadows.

"No!"

She shrieked at the top of her lungs, her skin all sweaty and clammy while she strained and struggled against the tangled web of sheets mostly in vain.

"Help me! Help!" she howled, her arms and legs feebly and powerlessly caught up flailing, punching, and kicking their way against the sheets that continued to squeezed around her, restricting her freedom.

"Esme! Ow! Stop it! Stop kicking!"

Bill's hoarse voice gradually brought her back from the land of sleep. This time, her arms ended up being pinned to her sides, his weight over her tenderized body forced her legs to stop kicking mostly out of the discoloring sore spots that were dispersed all over her body in the first place. Once more, Esme felt like a prisoner.

"Esme…"

"Don't touch me!"

Pain and anger viciously ripped themselves out of her throat, her voice squealing and feral. Slapping his hands away like a child having a tantrum, Esme started to cry her eyes and heart out until Bill stomped out of the room, rejected by his wife once and for all. Breathing heavily and weepily, she woke up beyond recall and reproach, lost and alone for the first time in her life. It was a strange vacant feeling, formed out of what one feels when one is lost and alone. Not a hopeful feeling on Esme's part, but one that promised to keep her alive and well for the rest of her life with any luck.

Which means…

"Bill."

Oh, how could she undoubtedly have wanted to shut out his name, but didn't because her voice got trapped inside her throat. How her lips formed his name to call for him, had she been silly enough to ignore all the pain he threw on and at her. Only the silence settled all around her, smothering her and her voice out of some hidden and well-meant safety.

Slinking away to the plushy comfort of his couch, Bill seethed at the panic-stricken rejection he had just gotten from Esme even though, technically, he applied great harm to her. His teeth grinding at full speed tension until he could taste his blood swirling in his mouth, he was within reach of his own personal opinion that he saved from his murderous intentions, rewarding her for her loyalty when due and this is the thanks she gets!

"How dare she!" Bill roared, slamming his right fist against the wall, causing the wall to give way around his fist, giving his knuckles cuts and splinters along the way.

How dare she!

His mind racing round and round itself at a wild frantic pace, anger hot and simmering beyond his control deep inside his pulsating veins and arteries. This is a dangerous time for Esme and him.

Esme…

How he literally would love to barge right into her room and throttle her senseless…or strangle her. No, he wouldn't strangle her. Telltale signs would lead the cops back to him and he already messed up with Amanda's strangulation. He tried to gas Esme, going so far as to make it look like she was hysterical and odd enough to lock herself up in the house and turned the gas on, as odd as it seemed. Because to him, it sounded like a good idea, one that could finally cut his ties to both sisters at once.

But he would do this, come hell or highwater.

Choosing to overlook his substantial amount of dismay and wonder at how Esme could have been so damned lucky to survive being gassed in her home until it hit him: Joanna. Of course, his wife would have a guardian angel in the form of her late sister!

Damn it!

He wanted to punch the walls and roar his anger and disappointment right at this moment, driving him into a fierce sort of determination that overrode his willing senses. Suddenly remembering the chloroform, he still had used on Amanda burning his left pocket, he carefully took out the chloroform and the handkerchief out of both pockets, he stole a deep breath to calm himself down and keeping himself in check as he added a big thoughtless splash of the remaining chloroform to the handkerchief, drenching it rather sloppily.

Delicately taking two stairs at a time, he stopped by Esme's door, the chloroform- saturated stinging and irritating his left hand more than he ever cared to admit as he crushed it in his hand. Without bothering to knock, Bill stole into the room with a simple soft click of the door's lock. Sitting with her back to him, Esme gave him the perfect opportunity to attack while she still had her head in her hands.

Perfect.

He congratulated himself as he noiselessly advanced up to her only to be betrayed by a squeaky floorboard or two. At the sound of his revealing footstep, his wife sat up and twisted her torso slightly and comfortably to face him, a wavering smile crossing her face, her voice shaky to a fault:

"Bill!"

Then more uncertainly:

"Bill?"

DECAY OF SORROW

Acting in a stealthy response, he stalked up to her, the chloroformed handkerchief burning his hand persistently, he stalked up to her with a treacherous impression of getting to her before pressing the handkerchief tight and firm against Esme's nose and mouth, shocking her with its recognizable sweet chemical-smelling scent and its strength scorching her skin a vivid inflamed redness. Once again that door reminded her of a doctor's office or clinic. As soon as she was forced unwillingly to inhale the fumes, a smarting headache immediately followed by this awfully spinning dizziness enveloping her whole, chasing her into freefalling down that long winding dark rabbit hole.

Captivated, Bill scrutinized with a keen eye at how her frenzied struggles unhurriedly drifted to nothingness, inviting him to ditch the handkerchief onto the floor and pick her up stupefied body in his arms. The minute she was secured in his arms, Bill risked a chance to take her back to the bathroom. Prudently positioning his unconscious wife in the dry bathtub as he feasibly can, he made sure that her feet and arms are tucked in the helpless poses so she could never get or help herself out ever again.

"Goodbye, Honey. It's been nice knowing you."

Twirling the taps on without any decisiveness on his part, he watched the water rush and cascade itself into the tub, a warm mini waterfall surging into the tub's vast beige porcelain-covered metal belly, casually over her clothed body and moving up past her head.

Spinning the faucet valves off, apparently pleased as punch that he will, at last, make Esme's death look like an accident, his only regret is not getting her to sign the insurance papers while she was alive. Oh, well, it's best to leave her to her own devices; in her case, drowning.

Locking the bathroom door with a sufficient twist of his right wrist, he casually tossed the key onto the coffee table once he sauntered down the stairs towards the couch. By the time he reached the couch, Bill definitely realized he had to act out for anyone who might be within earshot of the house's perimeter. He even flung open the windows for show!

"Damn it, Esme! Why can't you talk to me? Come on, Honey, stop sulking…"

Slamming doors, heavy stomping of feet, loud pounding of fists on doors and walls, and, finally, the last piece of this dog and pony show:

"Fine!"

Banging the front door closed behind him, Bill spun around and acted like he was checking the door to see if it was locked. Smiling to himself, he made sure that somebody—anybody—noticed what was going on between Esme and him so that somebody is interested enough to check on Esme and discover her body…maybe get caught as the murderer by Bill, the grieving husband himself.

"Everything okay, Mister Porcher?" a male voice that sounded as rich and deep as molasses called out to Bill's back, making him smile a wide grin, even more so than he imagined it achievable.

Todd! Of course! He will be the perfect patsy after that failed attempt with his sister…

Dropping his jubilant smile into a gloomy frown, Bill twirled around to face Todd. Todd, a nice helpful man whose name is that of a cartoon fox! Todd, the handsome man and employee.

Oh, how I hate Todd!

Bill being hopping mad, his icy blue eyes seeing that speedy explosion of vivid blood red, blinding him if only for a little while, his jealousy flowing hot and boiling through his veins.

"Yeah, everything's fine. Just a fight with Missus Porcher," Bill retorted, shrugging it off as unintentionally as he conceivably can.

"Is Esme…I mean, Missus Porcher…is she okay?"

He bristled with a possessive envy at how Todd took the liberty of saying Esme's first name, how actually concerned Todd was about Esme before answering, "Yes, Esme is okay. We just had a major fight. Couples do that. About money," adding that as if in afterthought.

"Oh" was all Todd could say even though he didn't downright believe the man. In his defense, he tried his best to sound convincingly sincere while still being believable despite not trusting anything Bill says at all in regards to Esme and her safety. To look like he, in fact, have confidence in Bill's words despite it being a less than stellar explanation. Then again Bill didn't need to offer any account at all except that Bill needed him for something, to be around until he is no longer essential. And one day, Todd knew that he will be Bill's fall guy one day.

The bathwater stirred and bubbled slowly but surely every time Esme breathed, drowning her little by little up until now when some invisible force gathered up enough strength and energy to lift Esme's torso and bent her over the rim in the same repetitious move as before. With hearty ghostly slaps on her back, Esme once again reacted to this lifesaving assertiveness by coughing up and heaving up water in what could only be a bucketful or two.

Gasping and choking, she sputtered and struggled for a lungful of air as she fought her way back from a watery grave. She was so busy straining for breath that she didn't notice being seized out of the bathtub ever so delicately as if she was a feather.

"Joanna?" Esme stammered before going into another hacking fit.

"Shh, just lay on your stomach and breathe. Slowly. In and out. I'm here, little sister. Do you have enough strength to get the rest of yourself out of the tub without my help?"

"I think I can."

"Please try."

"Okay."

On wobbly hands, feet, legs, and arms, Esme steadily pushed herself to try to reach for the floor, only to end up with her waterlogged clothes helping her to slip up and over the rim with a squishy wet splat. Curling up into a tight soaking wet shivering fetal ball, Esme stole a couple of minutes to rest before daring herself to get on her drenched hands and knees in a time-consuming, single-minded wriggle over to the door. With waterlogged fingers fumbling around the doorknob, trying to grasp it successfully and when she definitely got hold of that elusive knob, she turned it only to discover that it was locked.

"No…no…no!"

Scorching frantic tears welled in her eyes and fell down her pale cheeks as she tried once more to twist and turn, even pulling, that damned knob only to find it defying her every move even more so. Soundless tears developed into deep heaving sobs of "help" as the icy cold brutal awareness of being locked up in a prison to die slowly in if she lived, a watery grave of she died.

Accepting it useless and futile to knock and yell to get attention in an empty house as true, Esme was about to give up for good when something obviously caught her eye.

"The window!"

Pulling all her strength to put herself back onto her hands and knees, Esme carefully crept up to where the window is located: behind the tub. Still besieged to get all her faculties and strength together, she floundered in her attempts to pull the bathtub plug and make her move to open it.

"Come on…open for me…please," Esme howled as she gave it her best to pry open the window. After a few more tries, the window painstakingly threw itself open for her even though she almost fell backwards in the tub.

"Damn!" Esme bellowed as she fought with every inch of her willpower to steady herself, no longer caring if Bill hears her or not. "Help! Help me!"

"Esme?"

"Todd? Help me, please! I'm locked in and Bill tried to kill me—"

"Again?"

"Yes!"

"Hold on! I'm coming up, okay?"

Crying her heart out with tears of joy and gratefulness, she heard her knight in shining armor clamoring up the stairs, the heavy thudding of his feet being the best noise she has ever listened to as he eagerly kicked the bathroom door until it creaked, groaned, and cracked in protest before giving way to all of this abuse. Running up to her, Todd grabbed hold of Esme and pulled her close in a tight bear hug with firm gentle hands and great care.

Clinging to him like a drowning person clasping on to a life pre-server at sea, Esme certainly felt safe and protected.

"Todd…he…tried. To…kill…me…again…"

"Bill? I mean, Mister Porcher?"

"Yes."

It was all she could utter, her arms automatically tightened around his neck for dear life in response. Fear forcing her to shiver in reaction. All Todd could do was to squeezed his arms around her protectively and in kind, trying to wrap his head around what he had been correct about Bill Porcher all this time:

He tried to kill her for what? Insurance money?

"Now I want you to listen to me. Did you sign any papers? Insurance papers?"

He felt her shudder before she simply said, "I didn't sign them because he wouldn't let me read them."

"Good girl" was all he said into her hair, proud that she was smarter than he took her for granted. Kissing the top of her head, impossible and possible all in the same breath, Todd only knew of one place where Esme could be safe. Swinging her up into his arms, he simply growled:

"Come on."

"Where are you taking me?" Esme softly squeaked in his left ear, making him quiver in a strange pleasant way.

"Home," he pronounced while trying to keep his feelings and words under wraps, totally unaware that he rumbled the word "home" so low she must have misinterpreted it.

"No…*NO!* I don't want to be locked up in that bedroom ever again!"

"Locked in…wait. No, shh…I was talking about taking you to my cabin. <u>My</u> home," Todd soothed and cooed, blowing a sigh of relief as he felt her relax in his arms. For once in his life, Todd enjoyed playing the role of a hero who is both flawed and perfect. For once he was someone's hero, a knight in dented, dirt-stained armor.

Esme's hero.

"Esme?"

He realized she had already passed out in his arms, lost in a world of dreamless unconsciousness, making Todd more protective of the woman lying in his arms now more than ever.

Did he believe Esme about Bill?

It would have been easy to say both yes and no with the lines blurred in between because he was still crucial to Bill's plans. But then again, he was extremely going to great lengths to make sure Esme is safe and taken care of since she reminded him of Joanna, whom he developed a deep fondness for when the older sister was alive.

Deliberately depositing Esme in his bed, Todd studied her with a worried frown crossing on his handsome face.

How can I protect her from the likes of Bill? he wondered as he tenderly stroked her hair to reassure her as she dozed.

Twenty-Three

Bill took his time driving his car back to his house, hoping against hope to see the police arrest Todd for Esme's murder.

Almost there…

Turning the corner, Bill frowned in confusion at the sight of no police, no arrest, and no action. Perplexed and his ego a bit bruised, he parked his car in the driveway and turned off his car.

What the hell happened? He mouthed, sitting perfectly motionless inside his car and totally ignoring the growing heat slowly simmering deep inside his both him and his car.

Todd was supposed to be caught for Esme's murder!

Esme…

Getting out of the car as fast as he can by any means necessary, Bill locked its door more out of habit than necessity and slammed it shut. Stomping deliberately up the walkway, disappointment crept in his heart to stay minute by snail's pace minute. Reaching the front door, he swallowed up his intense disillusionment and turned the doorknob.

"Esme? Hello?"

Stillness greeted Bill like an old friend, giving him hope about inspiration, its atmosphere here inside his house comfortable and eerie in its vibe. His knee-jerk reaction was more of pure happiness mixed with something else. No, not sadness, concern, or any kind of grief, but more along the lines of unadulterated joy. Here in his house, he felt both safe and secure in his secret realization that he is such a bad man after all.

A bad man who had just killed his wife again.

Speaking of his wife…

Drawing near the spot on the coffee table, Bill expresses a sense of relief where he dropped the key earlier, the key was still there. Thrilled, he snatched up the key and killed some time downstairs before climbing up the steps towards the bathroom door without bothering to turn on the hall light. Strangely enough, the lock didn't give any resistance when he turned the key in it, something that should have raised alarms in his head, but didn't. The only thing that did caught his attention, disappointing him in turn, was there wasn't a wet floor or buckled floorboards *anywhere*. As he stood in front of the door in the darkness, his hand on the knob, he sucked in a deep breath, preparing himself for another death of another wife despite not feeling a damn thing for the whole situation.

It's just for show.

"Well, here goes nothing. Remember to play the grief-stricken widower, Bill," he reminded himself as he opened the door.

With a twist of the wrist and a flick of the light switch, he had to confess he was openly excited to see Esme deeply immersed in bathtub water.

But when he looked in the tub…

"Shit!"

The tub is empty!

The water…gone!

"Damn it! Where is she? Esme!"

He pulled the house apart from top to bottom, drastically yanking things and throwing things here and there in his search for her, never minding the fact that he missed the bathroom door jamb seemed to be splintered as if someone kicked the door in. The only thing that he risked noticing and deemed it out of place was the gaping bathroom window.

Bill, beyond a shadow of a doubt, got as far as the bathroom once again, his eyes casting a frosty stare all around the room until it discovered the slightly opened window above the tub.

"Damn it!" he howled at the top of his lungs, pounding his fists against the door jamb before turning his vicious attention to the wall in frustration and anger.

"Okay, Esme's gone. But where's Esme?"

He was about to fume some more when he realized that Esme was already in the coroner's and Todd was already in jail.

"Two birds, one stone," he purred, relieved he didn't have to clean up or act like the devastated widower until later when the police finally come to inform him with news about his late wife and Todd.

Twenty-Four

Esme slept dreamlessly and fitfully for the first time since this nightmare began. No ghostly sister to beg her to leave, no more deadly shadows with super sharp-edged knife-tipped fingernails clawing at her. No more circular spotlights to safely stand in. no more Bill to be afraid of.

"Esme…"

She bravely woke up to a soft male voice, deep and rich as a man's voice can get. Pleasant yet firm, kind and tender, his tone made her feel safe and, perhaps, even wanted.

"Esme."

His large hand, firm and gentle wrapped itself around her left shoulder, swallowing it whole. Friendly and even considerate, it absolutely insisted on shaking her awake.

"Come on, Esme."

"No, please let me sleep," she grumbled, trying her best to shudder his hand off just to be thwarted when his hand stubbornly pressed on in shaking her awake. "Must I?"

"Wake up? Yes. You need to eat some breakfast."

"Oh."

Cracking open her eyes, Esme saw a smiling handsome face to whom the voice belongs to.

"Todd?" she croaked, struggling weakly to sit up in the bed.

"Hello. Esme."

"Hi…where am I?"

"You are in my home…in my bed."

"Oh…okay. Did we…"

"Sleep together? No. I was the perfect gentleman and slept on the couch."

"Oh, okay."

"Is that all you have to say?"

Todd laughed this beautiful rich laugh that Esme had never heard before. Maybe it was because it sounded so real and genuine instead of Bill's fakeness. A laugh so sincere that it happened to coax Esme to relax and laugh right along with him. That is, before getting all too serious in the memory of what had just occurred to her.

"Todd, am I safe here?"

"Yes, you are."

He sat on the bed beside her, taking her hands in his in a tender reassuring gesture. For once, ever since she came to Meadoways, Esme felt protected and assured. A warm blush rose in her cheeks, its heat strongly pronounced in its own way, forcing her to drop her eyes down had it not been for Todd softly placing his hand under her chin, lifting it up so she can meet his eyes with hers.

"Do you hear me? You are safe here from him here."

"Okay. Thank you."

"You're welcome. I—"

A knock on the front door rudely broke off what he wanted to say to her, causing Todd to lose his train of thought much to his dismay.

"Hold that thought and hide, he ordered her, impulsively kissing her firmly and tenderly on the lips, rendering her breathless before leaving her in the bedroom with a soft click of the door closing.

"Okay," Esme softly called out to him, hoping he would have heard her as he closed the door. As a matter of fact, Todd certainly listened to her "okay" even though it was spoken rather faintly as he sauntered over to the front door. His front door, that is. Never minding the important question as to who would have the balls to come over here, to his house at this hour, Todd welcomed a smile playing on his lips with an awareness of his own making. Yet when he opened the door, that smile merely wiping itself away from his lips without warning as his eyes caught who he saw standing on his porch.

"Mister Porcher! What's going on?"

Was Todd imagining things or did he witness a hasty look of surprise and disappointment lurking deep inside the other man's icy blue stare? However, as soon as the look exposed itself, it was promptly blinked away as Bill piped up rather outrageously:

"Oh Todd! Thank God you are here. She's gone!"

"I'm sorry but who's gone?"

"Esme—Missus Porcher, I mean! She's disappeared as if into thin air!"

Shit! Did I remember to closed the bedroom door? Todd asked himself even as he politely let Bill in. A speedy scan of his eyes immediately reassured him the bedroom door is definitely closed and secured, much to Todd's contentment.

"Maybe she's gone out for a walk? It is a lovely day to go out walking."

"No, her things are gone, too…"

"Her things are gone? Hmm…"

Being an observant man, Todd stole a chance to rope in a closer glance at Bill's face without getting caught by the other man. At a pinched peek, Todd regarded the callous glint shining brightly and hard deep within the hidden icy depths of Bill's dry unemotional eyes. No sense of worry, no tears of loss. Just nothing. Even though Todd was an attentive man, he was more than surprised to see Bill had just lied to him without batting an eye because Esme is resting in his bedroom!

"Did you see Esme at all today?" did she say anything to you?" Bill probed, his eyes boring deep inside Todd's, expecting him to answer him just like his other employees. So, Todd gave the other man a response Bill might appreciate…or not:

"No, I was in my house all this time."

Discouragement danced a flurry pirouette in Bill's eyes once again, his voice hoarse and tired:

"Are you sure, Todd?"

"Yes. Yes, I am sure."

Of course, it was not true:

That he was in his house all day to the point he had to save Esme. It was also true about what Esme told him regarding Bill trying to kill her, that Bill essentially made this attempt seen with Todd's own eyes. What wasn't true was this mentioning of Esme's bags, of which Todd might have an idea about, but still didn't know about.

"Can I look around your house?"

"Sure, but why?"

"Well, just in case Esme—"

"Come here? Mister Porcher, she hadn't even been here or any of the other sections of this property. Plus, didn't you warn me not to mingle with your wife?"

"No, I don't remember that…"

"Okay, whatever. Come in. you are more than welcome to go through my house."

"I know, but…"

"You need to know."

"Yes."

Stuck between wanting to protect Esme and wanting to kick Bill Porcher out of his home, Todd had to bite his tongue and allow the other man to search through his cabin since he already told Bill that he hadn't seen Esme at all.

"Go ahead, just don't rifle through my things, okay?"

Bill looked offended, his voice sounding just as hurt as the man's ego:

"I don't have time to rifle, Todd. I just need to see if Esme snuck in here without you knowing."

"But why me? Esme doesn't know me at all."

"True, but it doesn't hurt, right?"

Torn between laughing like a maniac and bellowing out in frustration, Todd didn't have much choice or any reason to stop the other man, no matter what he felt or thought otherwise.

"Go on, sir, I got things to do."

"Thank you, Todd."

Todd diplomatically waved away the gratitude, feeling like a heel for betraying Esme this way. Right now, it would have been easy to say he is wedged between a rock and a hard place. It would have been a lie, of course. He could have been brave and stand up to Bill, tell him "no" when asked to go through his house for any signs of Esme, but didn't.

"Mister Porcher…"

Bill wandered up to the first bedroom door. With his hand on the doorknob, he turned to Todd, a confused look crossing his face and eyes.

"What?"

"Nothing."

"Are you sure?"

"Yes…yes, I am."

Shrugging it off as if it was nothing, Bill twisted the knob without any fanfare and pushed open the door. Much to Todd's dismay or maybe to his surprise, Bill sauntered in only to come out as swiftly as he went in. puzzled, Todd snuck into his bedroom while the other man checked out the other rooms, including another bedroom, and found…

Nothing and nobody.

"Thanks, Todd, for letting me look for her here," Bill shouted out to Todd from the front door.

"Yeah, no problem," Todd sputtered with an absentminded wave of his right hand, his shocked mind completely at a loss as to what the hell happened to Esme.

At the severe crash of the front door brought Todd back from his state of shock, a small feminine voice piping up from out of nowhere, scaring him for a brief moment:

"Is he gone?"

"Esme? Esme! Where are you?"

"Under the bed."

As if on cue, a petite hand shot out, asking for him to gently but firmly grab and pull her out from underneath the bed. With a fire in his belly and under his butt, Todd rushed over to calmly yet determinedly grasp her outstretched hand and pluck her carefully free from her hiding place.

"Thank you."

"So, he didn't see you?"

"Bill? Almost. Twice, in fact."

"Twice?"

"Yeah, twice. Bill seemed pretty quick in his so-called 'searching'. Sometimes he was just stand there and did nothing," Esme answered back matter-of-factly.

"Oh."

Esme grinned a sheepishly enigmatic smile at him, making Todd feel as though she knew what he was thinking about immediately. A beautiful Mona Lisa smile, he swears, made Todd fall in love with Joanna's younger sister.

A married woman!

Woah, woah, I love Esme, yes, I do.

With those thoughts dancing a lively little jig deep inside his head, Todd smiled right at Esme, his smile just as bright and warm if not brighter and warmer than hers even though it is not as embarrassed nor mysterious as hers.

"Todd?"

"Yes?"

"What do we do now?"

"We got to get you out of here as fast and safely as we can, he claimed, ignoring the sharp pain ripping through the extremely pounding core of his heart.

"And then what?"

"Good question."

It was truthfully a good question, one Todd didn't think he would ever hear, the knife-edged throes slashing and cutting within the heavy depths of his heart ebbing and flowing all at once. He accurately didn't want to bargain for all of these feelings and such. Nevertheless, it was a query that had never crossed his mind. A question that shouldn't cause him any worry, but still do for the first time in his life.

"We really need to get you out of here without Mister Porcher seeing or knowing, he repeated with more conviction.

"Mister Porcher?"

"Bill."

"Oh."

If Todd didn't listen to her so sensibly, he would have certainly missed the soft appreciation swaying in her voice. He did and it delighted him greatly. In fact, his heart also took up to frolicking as well.

"Now, as far as what we can do to get you out of Dodge without Bill seeing or noticing, he echoed while burying himself in contemplation.

"How?"

"That I don't know…yet."

"Well, we should start now before Bill finally figures it out and comes back."

"Esme, do you think he will come back?"

"Of course, because I am a loose end…*oh*."

"And he needs to tie up all the loose ends, including yourself?"

'Right."

At a certain precise moment, Todd didn't easily know how or even what to feel other than a whole chunk of protectiveness mixed in with a bit of sadness, along with some fear and discontent. He honestly wanted Esme to stay. On the other hand, he grasped deep in his heart that it is too dangerous for her to stay with him.

"Well, Todd?"

"Hmm…I'm thinking…"

Esme is betwixt and between laughing and crying as she patiently waited for him to think up something. Something out of harm's way, she supposed, on the grounds of the danger outside in the shape of Bill Porcher. With a heavy and disenchanted heart, she admittedly hated the idea of leaving Todd to deal with Bill by himself and leaving Todd for parts unknown.

"I got it! We will have to do this late at night, so I think it might work," Todd reacted with a snap of his strong fingers and a huge grin on his lips. At the sight of his smile, Esme envisioned she might melt away into a quivering puddle of warm gooeyness at any minute.

"Okay."

She winced at her one-word reply on the grounds it simply shrieks "stupid girl" in her ears once it rolled off the tip of her tongue. Suddenly Esme suffered from shame and shyness, wishing she was beautiful and smart and perky instead of being a silly stupid mouse who ends up being tongue-tied around Todd and his smart and caring and handsome self.

"What's wrong?"

"I—nothing."

Esme politely gesticulated away her ridiculous thought before it had a chance to escape from her lips. Then again maybe she should have said it, let it run off by rolling off the tip of her tongue, apart from the fact she had completely forgotten it now.

"So, what's the plan?"

Todd smiled that knee-melting grin, making Esme's knees tremble deliciously and her cheeks flush a sweet innocent blush like a certain schoolgirl towards her crush instead of a grown woman.

Oh, how I love his smile, she considered with a nervous smile as she stole peeks at him when she was certain that he wasn't looking. He was huskier than Bill, but he was sexy and handsome than Bill. Even at a closer look, he was more human than a god, something that made Esme sigh in comfort.

"I'll think of something, Esme."

"Promise, Todd?"

"Promise."

Twenty-Five

The night dared itself to roll in quietly and quickly just as Todd dreaded the idea of letting Esme go. The truth is this: he didn't want to let Esme go. Not now and definitely not ever. He knew it has been such a short time between them, but he cared about her in so many ways despite knowing that she is someone's wife.

"This is crazy…hell, *I'm* crazy…"

He muttered to himself, not caring he is talking to himself in his guest bed in the middle of the night. Being the perfect gentleman, Todd made sure he stayed that way just in case Esme didn't feel the same way as him.

Over in her temporary bed, Esme was motionless in a pain-staking sort of way, trying her best to keep the night from arriving only to be too little, too late. As a result, she began to cry huge tears of sadness and disenchantment like a child who didn't get her way and got spanked instead. Unlike a child, she understood the danger of staying here, but like a child, she wanted to stay.

Esme stifled a sob as she urged a wordless prayer to break from her heart, shattering it into a million sharp little pieces. Sure, she has only known Todd for a sort time and not that well. However, this short amount of time has become something special to her even though they merely met and talk to each other not that much.

"I wish Joanna would talk to me again. She would have all the answers to my questions and help me."

By being a twin, Esme kind of figured it out such supernatural things, like hearing her late sister's voice inside her head, can be flukes of nature in addition to things that survived outside the normal box.

At least that is what she knows about ghosts…

A soft knock on the bedroom door burst through her thoughts, forcing Esme to rub her eyes with the backs of her hands so hard that she could see stars frolicking behind her closed eyelids.

"Yes?" she asked, breathlessly frightened that it might not be Todd.

"It's Todd. Can I come in?"

"Yes."

Todd's stomach dropped and flipped so many times he stopped counting as she strolled in the room and saw her sitting crossed legged smack dab in the middle of the bed, cheerlessly staring at him with red puffy eyes.

"You have been crying."

"No, I haven't. it's just allergies."

"Liar."

He smiled a kind and loving smile when he said it, his left hand tenderly and attentively caressing her left cheek, perhaps a bit longer than anticipated. Oh, if only they were in a different time and place, they would have definitely been together romantically and beyond.

"Are you ready to go, Esme?"

"Yes."

No, her mind screamed at her. Esme simply shrugged off the one-word protest as promptly as she possibly could.

"Let's go, Esme. If I am right, you will be safely away from here and Bill in a couple of hours or so, okay?"

"Okay."

As hurriedly and silently as she is capable of, Esme put on her clothes and shoes while Todd had his back to her. Once she is completely dressed, she softly called out "done" to Todd's back, he turned around and smiled before she followed him out the bedroom and into the barely lit living room. With the hall light on, the eerie buttery yellow glow cast all around the cabin as far as the light can reached and cannot spread. Stretching out his large hands, Todd barely contained his joy once Esme gently placed her petite hands in his.

"Ready, Esme?"

"Ready."

They just stood there, unaware of the time and the heavy shadow lurking and passing the windows here and there, a restless fury pulsating at this one window, catching Esme's eye as she screamed out to Todd:

"Todd, look out!"

Without any warning, the shadowy humanoid figure threw itself against the window, crashing through like an awkward swashbuckler as the window's glass rained and showered the living room, Esme, and Todd. Screeching in horror, Esme could only stand frozen in terrible fear and hopelessly watch the human figure come up from behind Todd and struck him down in one swoop of its long arm. Frightening her into running back to the comfort and safety of the bedroom when she heard the booming shout as she slammed the door:

"Esme!"

"Bill…"

Locking the door as quick as her right wrist can flick the lock, she fought to worm her way under the bed as hastily as she feasibly can, bumping her head, legs, and arms on the bed frame. Minutes later, she caught the sound of a body smashing forcefully against the door in thuds, creaks and cracking. It was the door being destroyed, breaking her down to shriek out in horror as Bill charged in.

"Esme! He bellowed, his tone firm and breathless and ordering, demanding her to answer him.

In absolute terror, Esme slapped her hands over her mouth to quell her heavy breathing and anguished sobs. She knew she was failing because Bill caught her by the ankles, dragging her kicking and screaming from under the bed.

"No! *No!*"

"Got you! Now shut up!"

Smacking her hard across the face, stunning her into an unconscious silence, Bill flung her over his right shoulder, hauling her out of Todd's cabin, her head bobbing between consciousness and unconsciousness, never to see if Todd was okay or not. Flashes of time and tiny bits of scenery sailing by as minutes altered into hours then something else, she couldn't even fathom right now. Later on, Esme found herself unable to fight back when she Bill locked his arms around her, trapping her arms in a tight embrace.

"Please, Bill. Please let me go. I promise I won't run away."

"No, Esme. I did that with you before and you ran away. No more."

"I'll be good! Please! Please let me live!"

Climbing up the stairs, Bill stopped for one fleeting moment, giving Esme hope in spite of her aching head until she heard the snarl coming out of him:

"You're just like your sister. Too naïve, too stubborn, and a damned pain in the ass! Your sister…that bitch was too mulish to die until I finally got her to drink that tea made from the Lilies of the Valley water. And don't get me started on Amanda!"

"What did you do to Amanda?"

"Killed her, of course, because she was so greedy and you weren't. but then again, I should have made you signed those insurance papers. My money's running low."

Esme shuddered at how calm and calculating he sounded as he made a fruitless attempt to laugh at his poorly made joke. Then again, Esme wasn't too sure if he was joking or not. With one arm tight around her waist, he whipped out some rope from out of nowhere, at least from her standpoint, before dragging her up the remaining stairs. With one eager kick, the door swung open and he flung her onto the tiled bathroom. Landing with a bruising thump, bringing about more bruises upon bruises on her body, Esme laid perfectly still while the pain in her head and on her body grew too excruciating to stand. Her breathing shallow and sometimes even, she willed herself to calm down while her mind raced around all this derangement coming from everywhere Bill goes.

If I crawl on my belly…

Blinded by the pain, in her head and all over her body, Esme prayed for her fingers, arms, legs, and feet to function as she strived to scramble to lie on her belly and gingerly pull herself along in order to get out of the bathroom. Slowly but surely, she clambered her clumsy way, bruised and injured, until she reached the edge of the stairs. Behind her she could hear the water running, telling her what he planned to do next to her, taking a deep breath, all she could mumble was:

"Here goes nothing."

Dragging herself over the top stair, she experienced she was chaotically being thrown all over the place, crashing and flipping, sometimes head over heels, sometimes rolling, the pain intensified all over the place on her body, hitting her head from time to time until she thought—or hoped—that she landed on the bottom of the stairway. Whimpering ever so softly, Esme called out for her sister to come and get her out of this predicament:

"Joanna…"

"Oh, Esme…you looked terrible…"

"He's going to kill me for real this time, Joanna. No turning back."

"Not if I have my way."

Esme sensed her heart lifting just a little bit at the sound of her older sister's vow to protect her prattled on inside her head, compelling her to worry about something else:

"Joanna, I'm so very scared. I don't want to die."

"I know and you won't little sister. Not on my watch."

"What should I do?"

"Lie still, Esme. More than that, you are in too much great pain to fight him. Okay?"

"Okay."

"Shh…Bill's coming."

Tears burned her eyes and stained her cheeks as her ears heeded the rough and thumping noises of bill running down the stairs, his voice giving her a lecture as he clambered downstairs:

"Esme! Oh Esme! What the hell do you think you're doing? This isn't what I visioned and now you might have more bruises—no, wait. It's perfect. I will lose a house, but it will be wonderful!"

Bill's hooting and hollering injured her ears as she wondered just what he is planning on doing with her. Not that she literally cared, but something was concerned about her.

"Come here, my bruised beauty!" he squawked as he swept her up into his arms and sauntered over to one of the dining room chairs, he pulled out for himself before this drama began. Standing on the tabletop is a vase of the Lilies of the Valley. Sitting her down in the chair, Bill whooped a little bit too smug, too proud for his ego to waste:

"You see the Lilies of the Valley, Esme? This time I didn't throw them away."

Staring at the flowers, she found her voice, her defiance louder than the words she declared:

"So, you're the one who put them on the table to do what? Taunt me? Frighten me?"

Confusion struck him dumb, making him stammered:

"Huh? No."

"Then who did, Bill?"

"I don't know."

She caught the hidden tremble in Bill's voice and relished it. For once, her husband is not in total control. In a slight moment, Esme experienced a bravery so strong that she no longer feared Bill's threats of her dying at *his* hands.

Good. Let him stew, she judged airily, feeling ever so safe and secure in her flash of courage.

Her heart fluttered and paused with anxiety and excitement. Has she saved her own life even if only for a little while?

"Stop it! Stop it! Stop looking at me like that! There is nothing wrong with me!" Bill yelped at the topo of his lungs; his voice hoarse with emotion. "*You* are the one who is not getting out alive!"

Once again Esme felt her heart rapidly beat a fierce tattoo as she wondered:

Now what can I do to keep myself alive? If only for a little while, she promised herself.

Bill is going irrational right now. The vase of the Lilies of the Valley still stood there pm the dining room table, defiant as they were, the strange pity looks coming from Esme. Now he must tie his wife up with the rope he acquired from one of the curtains in the living room.

"Shut up!"

Esme didn't say a word nor did she plan to say a word to Bill out of anxiety and terror. Nor did she cried out in pain when the rope he tied on and around her ankles and wrists burned deep into her skin.

"There."

Bill sounded both amused and determined all at the same time, scaring Esme.

"There."

He repeated the word with a dull readiness in a frightening ease. Causing her to feel her heart to drop down into her stomach and settle there, making her both nauseated and under the weather all at once.

"There."

She sincerely started to hate this word with a passion. His constant repetition of "there" as if he was ridiculing her fear with this word one uses for comfort. That word "there" began to grate on her nerves, callously tearing and shredding her heart and soul apart.

"Stop it! Stop it!" she screamed to the ceiling, fruitlessly writhing against the taut stretched rope, driving the rope to carve deeper and tighter into her thrashed skin, the pain totally pissing her off.

"Shut up, Bill!"

Hard as a brick, his open-palmed hand hurled across her silky bruised left cheek along with the left side of her mouth so impenetrable and cruel that she was literally aware of the fresh metallic mouthful of blood flowing in and all over her once delectable mouth. Commanding her to cry out, spewing droplets of her vital fluid connecting to the table in turn.

"Look what you made me do! Are you happy? Tell me! Are you happy?" he roared, spitting out those words into her banged up and bleeding face, his body priming itself into landing another round of blows on her unprotected body and soul, ready to strike at will without any provocation once again. Violently shaking her wounded head to deny him the right to smack her in addition to clearing her head, she tried her best to quickly disregard the sharp pain slashing through her head and body even as she fell back into silence once more, hoping that this wrecked peace will last a little longer for her life's sake.

"Good girl."

Bill lightly patted her head like she was some pet or a good little girl who cleaned up her room as told. Esme obviously blanched at his touch. If Bill noticed this, he didn't let it show.

"Good girl. Maybe if you're good enough, I will let you live," he drones on, still caressing her blood matted hair. Esme, for her part, wasn't certain that her head had been split opened, except that she was a complete mess from all the abuse Bill has given her. By now she relaxed a little while still on some kind of alert, her head and body protesting something fierce.

"Bill?" she slurred; unaware she said his name out loud as she traveled in and out of consciousness.

"What?" he demanded, his body tense with unspoken anger, ready to strike at any minute.

"Never mind. I forgot."

Truth be known, thanks to her weak and foggy mind, she certainly did let whatever she wanted to say slip from her lips as a result from her memory of Bill going off on her again.

Yes, it was safer for her to forget.

"Esme…"

"Joanna? Where are you?"

"Close."

"How close?"

"Closer than you think."

As if on cue, the vase of the Lilies of the Valley knocked itself down, spilling both the flowers and their water across the table's shiny surface, spreading like a giant puddle or a massive bloodstain by the way it stretches.

"No…no…*no*! What did you do?"

This time Bill slugged her with an outraged closed right fist. Now her right cheek stinged and throbbed, her right ear ringing something godawful, and her right eye swelled into a goose egg from the rapid walloping she got from her husband. Her tears smarting and searing her eyes, she tried her best to blink them away so Bill wouldn't have the chance to see her crying.

"Are you okay, Esme?"

I'm okay, Joanna, just in so much pain.

Esme made sure that she mentally spoke her words out to her sister, eager for Joanna to hear her speak telepathically with her. It didn't take too long for Esme to get her answer from Joanna:

"Want me to do something to him?"

But you're ghost. How can you do anything to him?

"Oh, I have my ways, little sister."

With her ear screaming, cheeks and body burning and throbbing in concentrated agony, Esme cringed in pure terror at the idea of Bill coming near her again with the full intent of hurting her. Striving for her best to catch where Bill is located, she grew anxious and frustrated as a result of this maltreatment.

Where's Bill?

Watching the dining room tabletop, Esme immediately noticed something else:

Hey, where's the vase of the Lilies of the Valley?

As if to answer her silent question, a vase of the Lilies of the Valley abruptly smacked down on top of the table, its water sloshing precariously in its vase.

"Like I said, your sister was hard to kill, so I had to improvise and do my research When she was sick, I gave a cup of hot tea made with the water that the Lilies of the Valley were soaking in. Then again, I didn't beat the living tar out of her like I did with you," he laughed a cruel heartless chuckle before going on, "You see, the Lilies of the Valley are poisonous flowers. Hell, even the water that they soak in is toxic! Just simply take the flowers out of the vase and—voilà—you have poisonous water. This water here," he announced with a gentle nudge of the vase towards her, "can cause you to have a heart attack or an appearance of one, I can't remember. Either way, you will end up dying of a 'heart attack' just like your sister…and I will play the role of the grieving husband! This time they will not have the audacity to suspect me like they did with my other wives—oops! I didn't mention that I had other wives—including you, I say about five. Yes, five wives. Doesn't that shock you?"

"Bastard."

Esme bit the inside of her cheek hard to keep herself from screaming while Joanna's "bastard" insult fell on deaf cars. Bill's deaf ears, that is.

Bill killed Joanna…he confirmed it! Esme's intellect screeched at its highest zenith. It was the confirmation that brought Esme back to this world and lifetime. Joanna told her the truth! Now, she understood why her older sister was trying to save her from Bill. This shocking realization fetched her back from giving up to now fighting for her life.

"You bastard," Esme spat out at him, furiously listening helplessly to Bill's laughter, mocking her callously.

"What are you going to do? Beat me up while you're all tied up?" he howled, nearly choking on his own spittle as he laughed.

"I wish," Esme growled under her breath, glaring at him.

Bending down to meet her topaz defiant stare, Bill smirked right at her, his voice sarcastic and cruel:

"Hmm…so much courage for someone who is about to die."

Esme tried to squirm, but the rope made it faultlessly impossible for her to do so. Helpless, she sat awfully still, defeated and alone, seething in total quietness.

"No brave smart words, wife?"

She shook her head in response.

"Oh, Esme…"

I'm afraid that I'm at a disadvantage, Joanna. I will see you soon.

For once, Joanna appeared to be at a loss for words, causing Esme worried and anxious in a heartbeat.

"Let's get started, hmm?" Bill hummed, his eyes shining bright with a devilish glee.

Placing a clean glass right in front of Esme, Bill cautiously piked up the Lilies of the Valley out of their vessel. With a tangible trepidation, Esme watched with fear-filled eyes as he poured the vase water into the glass, no filter, with a careful and deliberate consideration.

"I apologize for the dirty water, but I need to kill you before I set the house on fire," he gloated over her before methodically taking his time sitting in a chair beside her, over at her left side. "What a perfect wife you could have been, but you were always too much, too meddling, right? Yes, meddling…not too much but enough to bring us here. Too stubborn for me…just like you sister. Hell, you even look like her!"

"That's because we're identical twins," Esme muttered under her breath.

"What's that?" he asked almost too innocently as he smoothly pushed the glass of vase water towards Esme.

"You scare me."

"Scare you? Why should I scare you, my brave stubborn wife?"

Bill reached out to stroke her bruised left cheek, inducing her to scream and cry out in painful agony as he persistently poked and prodded her raw aching cheek. An overflowing of frenzied watery tears spilling themselves in cascades at the same time he laughed gleefully at her pain and torment in cold blood.

"Aww…poor Esme…what should I do with you?" Bill teased rather maliciously as he bent over her.

"Please…Bill…it…hurts," she gasped out in discomfort. He laughed a snarky chuckle, mocking her and her pain in a high-pitched squeaky version of her voice before lowering to his normal tone. "You know why I married you? I had to get it right the second time. It wasn't about love, just to get it right. But since it didn't end up the way I wanted it to be, now it's time for you to drink the vase water."

"No."

"Sorry?"

"I said 'No.'"

Grabbing the back of the chair, Bill leaned Esme back so far, she could feel the heart-numbing fear of falling, forcing a terrified wheeze to escape from the lips.

"Well, you don't have much of a choice, do we? Drink," he snarled. "Boy, you *are* heavy!"

He aimed to harm her, to insult her, to get under her skin and inside her head in order to get her to drink the damn vase water. In fact, he made his point by dropping her chair a couple of bone-jarring inches. She squealed once again in response.

"No!"

"Drink it…"

"No."

"Drink!"

Bill released her chair onto the floor, making her yelp in pain as the back of her head bounced like a rubber ball. Stunned and in sheer agony, Esme wasn't able to find her senses to fight any more, allowing him to tightly pinched her nose, forcing her to breathe through her mouth, granting Bill the opportunity to pour the vase water down her throat. Overpowered, coughing and sputtering, Esme managed to fought back by spitting up and spewing out the water as immediately as she possibly can.

All the while Bill sneered with glee:

"Silly Esme! Don't you know that you are already poisoned! This poison is quick and your heart should start seizing right… about…now!"

As if to prove her husband's point, a deep sharp pain struck her hard right in the center of her heart, snatching her heart's muscles in a tight embrace, gripping it tightly over and over again, frightening her just as he picked her up and carried her up the stairs.

To the bathroom.

"No…"

"This time you will finally be a drowning victim. I hope you don't mind me telling you this. I will reveal to the police that you have a heart attack and fell in the tub to your death, so they can call the ambulance. I will play the mourning husband, of course, a good role to be in especially once I find someone to take your place."

"You…ow…bastard…"

"Now, now. Is that how you should talk to your widower?" he tsked as he casually plopped her gently into the tub full of water, the action causing her to hit the back of her head on the porcelain, bringing on the stars to flash and dance before her stunned eyes.

Help me, Joanna, please.

She pleaded inside her achy head prior to the darkness sweeping up to swallow her whole as she slipped under the water. When holding her breath proved to be futile, she started to gasped and fight against the water's persistent insistence to flow right into her mouth and nose as if it was nothing to worry about. Watching all of this, Bill took the time to carefully cut off the rope as he stood over her, his soon-to-be late wife, staring at her as if she was some interesting work of art.

"Good bye, Esme."

In her pain-riddled heart, she wanted to yell "no!" one last time as her lungs began to fill up with water, causing her to struggle even more so as she fought somewhat valiantly to her death. besides the sheer agony wouldn't allow it as he turned on his heel and walked out of the bathroom as if nothing was happening at all…

No…

Esme disagree wholeheartedly.

Reviewing her troubles right now, she is dying, left alone in a bathtub full of water, while he, her so-called husband., is concocting some story about how he found her lying there or something close to it inside his narcissistic head. Her body tired and weak from the poisoning and the intense pain from beatings, Esme decide to take a chance and try to get herself out of here. Fumbling and slipping, she bungled and flailed helplessly for a minute before she turned and her right arm flung itself over the rim. Overjoyed with this successful attempt, never mind how minor it is and was, she painfully dragged herself up to finally get her head above water. Pleading at the top of her lungs, damning the pain:

"Help. Me…"

Pull up, Esme mentally ordered her muscles. Even though they protested to a certain extent, she was amazed to learn that they achingly obeyed, pulling her lethargic torso up and over the rim with some kind of supernatural strength despite recognizing it was her will to live that was pushing herself to do these things. She trembled with strain as she pushed herself further over the rim, seeing the tiled floor for the first time in minutes or hours, she no longer cared. With one more final drive to safety, Esme actually threw up water as she landed on the tiled floor with a sickening thud. Scared and all alone, she shivered violent as she purged the water out of her lungs, completely aware of the opened door only a few steps away from her.

"Help…me…" she breathed and coughed out loud, not worrying about all this noise bringing Bill back upstairs. Wheezing with difficulty as she rolled prudently onto her stomach, she crawled towards the bathroom door as fast as her arms and feet could carry her, her seizing heart pounding a fierce tattoo, hurting her in spasms and twists while struggling to breathe and live.

"Help…me."

Landing only a couple of steps away from the top of the staircase, Esme drifted in and out of awareness for what seemed to be like an eternity when Todd's voice blew in through her fuzzy foggy haze:

"Esme! Esme! Can you hear me?"

"Todd…Todd? I'm poisoned…my heart it hurts…Lilies of the Valley…Bill did it…heart attack…"

The next thing she knew was that she passed out in a pair of warm, strong arms.

Twenty-Six

Proceeding as if nothing happened, not heeding the activity happening at top of the stairs or down here in the first floor, Bill went about energetically cleaning up the dining room table, whistling a happy tune as he threw away the flowers and washing the glass and vase. All done without a devil may care attitude even as he towel-dried the glass and vase.

"Bastard!" shrieked an echo that seemed more like Joanna's voice from here. There, and everywhere deep within the darkened depths of his house in a frantic case of brazenness, bouncing off the walls before reaching Bill's ears. The resonance causing him to drop both the glass and vase on the floor with an earsplitting cacophony of crashes and tinkles.

"Who's here? answer me!" he yowled out of uncontrolled fear, his eyes scanning here, there, and all over the place in a frenzied possession

An uncontrollable giggle washed and overwhelmed him, smacking him down personally in a kind of phobic fear as the whole house vibrated and fastened its doors and windows from top to bottom, frightening Bill right where he stood. On the other hand, he recognized that giggle all too well, from anywhere except he had forgotten so easily when he married Esme.

"Joanna, I don't believe in ghosts and the supernatural and I certainly don't believe in you!" he squawked at the top of his lungs, its echoes bouncing off the walls and floors so quickly that it could have made his head spin, knowing that he lied when he addressed her, his late wife.

As if to defy him in outrage and answer him all at once, the lights all over the house began to flicker excitedly on and off while an icy wind whizzed throughout the house's vulnerable rooms, knocking things over, breaking things, and throwing thing at Bill, who raced all over the house, trying with all his might to open every door and every window he had access to. Running to the dining room in a frantic state, his horror-saturated eyes spotted the defiant sight of the Lilies of the Valley poised ever so beautifully right there on the dining room table.

Bill hollered out at the flowers, hating what a scene they have become to him.

"Ah! Leave me alone!"

He dashed all over the house, staggered by fright and irrationality, all the while the haunting continued. Somehow along the way during these chaotic noises, the gas on the stove clicked itself on, its blue flames fanned out during the process. Without any warning, a soft whooshed of a match striking its box, creating a good-sized blaze to throw onto the stove, drawing Bill to it like a moth to a flame.

"Oh shit" was all Bill could say before the eager flames danced together and morphed into one huge explosion of a conflagration, ravenously eating both Bill and the house up once and for all.

Twenty-Seven

"Wake up, Esme. You're safe and free. And now I'm set free too."

Esme mumbled something unintelligible in order to protest her sister's happy-sounding farewell while in the process of struggling to wake up. For her, it seemed so final as the thought of her older sister leaving her to go to Heaven or the Great Unknown as some like to call it. She really didn't want to lose Joanna, much less let Joanna go…and that she couldn't control.

"Missus Porcher? Time for your medicine," a female voice gently poked and prodded her aching mind back to the here and now. Muttering another inarticulate gripe, Esme finally cracked open her eyes wide in wakefulness.

"Where am I?"

"You're in the hospital. You are very lucky. We were afraid that you weren't going to make it because you were stable one minute, critical the next. The reason was due to the poison that was given to you."

"I was poisoned."

She already knew that she was poisoned. She remembered Bill tossing the dirty vase water down her throat and try to drown her before passing out. Yet the nurse didn't seem to notice that it wasn't a question, her voice soft and caring:

"Yes…according to the gentleman—your husband—who was with you when—"

"My husband? He's here?"

Worry and fear churned around in her heart and stomach, sweeping over her, her topaz eyes scanning for quick places to hide when he comes in as well as for signs of him. Finding nothing, Esme relaxed to a point before recalling the only man who took great care of her:

"What about Todd?"

"Todd?"

"Yes, tall, handsome, amazing hazel eyes, husky built, golden tan skin, caring…ring a bell?"

"Sorry, I didn't see him. We do know that you were poisoned by the flowers called the Lilies of the Valley. Luckily, the doctor knew what to do to handle your situation."

Disappointed, Esme decided to look around her room from her bed. The hospital room appeared warm and inviting while still smelling like a hospital. Its walls painted a cool pale yellow that grew strangely warm by the light of the sun. a nice small room but comfortable all the same.

"Thank you."

The nurse looked confused, her voice betraying her so:

"For what, Missus Porcher?"

"For saving me," Esme replied meekly while taking her prescribed medicine with a tentative sip or two of water before gulping it down.

"What kind of medicine is this? that I'm taking, I mean?"

"The medicine to help your heart. Your heart might have some damage to your heart."

The doctor who came in to informed her about her medicine looked like a kind grandfather who chose to heal and take care of the sick instead. His voice, kind and gentle, was especially made to soothe patients' fears even with the bad news.

"Hello, I'm Dr. Artemis and I am going to be your doctor while you're in the hospital."

Dr. Artemis, being the perfect professional in his field, took her pulse, listen to her heart, and check her heart rate. Nodding as if pleased with the results.

Dr. Artemis promised:

"Your vitals are good. I will be back tomorrow. You are getting better, which is something I hoped for. Okay?"

"Okay, doctor."

"Now we have to let you rest. You also have a visitor, but make sure that you rest, hmm?"

"Todd! You're alive!"

"Just for you, Esme. And with Joanna's help."

"Joanna? What did she do?"

"She opened the front door for me when I was carrying you out of the house."

"So, you are not a ghost?"

"Nope."

"What about Bill?"

"Bill died in the fire. I'm sorry."

"Is it bad to say that I'm not?"

"If he treated you differently, then yes. But since he didn't…"

He shrugged his shoulders while Esme drawled:

"I understand."

"What about our future, Esme? What should we do about that?"

"*Our* future? Does that mean—"

"You and me together? Why not? That is, if you have me."

"Yes, yes, of course!"

"Now the doctor says that you must rest. So, please rest and when you get better, we can start our life together, okay?"

"Okay."

Epilogue

A couple of weeks later, Esme sauntered into her therapist's office, feeling better and a little scarred as a result of Bill's abusive brutality. On the other hand, she and Todd are still going on strong and so her heart and life are in a better condition. Marriage might come to mind, but Esme and Todd aren't in a rush except to come home to each other and love each other with as much passion and love as they can deliver to each other. She is about as perfectly happy as she can be, most likely even more so, now that Todd is here with her.

Taking a seat in a chair opposite her therapist's, Esme stole a deep breath and relaxed, her voice alive and happy:

"Okay, I am ready to talk."